The Case of the Itinerant Ibizan

A Thousand Islands Doggy Inn Mystery

B.R. Snow

Copyright © 2017 B.R. Snow

ISBN: 978-1-942691-30-3

Website: www.brsnow.net/

Twitter: @BernSnow

Facebook: facebook.com/bernsnow

Cover Design: Reggie Cullen

Cover Photo: James R. Miller

Other Books by B.R. Snow

The Thousand Islands Doggy Inn Mysteries

- The Case of the Abandoned Aussie
- The Case of the Brokenhearted Bulldog
- The Case of the Caged Cockers
- The Case of the Dapper Dandie Dinmont
- The Case of the Eccentric Elkhound
- The Case of the Faithful Frenchie
- The Case of the Graceful Goldens
- The Case of the Hurricane Hounds

The Whiskey Run Chronicles

- Episode 1 – The Dry Season Approaches
- Episode 2 – Friends and Enemies
- Episode 3 – Let the Games Begin
- Episode 4 – Enter the Revenuer
- Episode 5 – A Changing Landscape
- Episode 6 – Entrepreneurial Spirits
- Episode 7 – All Hands On Deck
- The Whiskey Run Chronicles – The Complete Volume 1

The Damaged Posse

- American Midnight
- Larrikin Gene
- Sneaker World
- Summerman
- The Duplicates

Other Books

- Divorce Hotel
- Either Ore

To Summer

Chapter 1

I guess four o'clock in the morning, softly lit by a full moon, is as good a time as any to do a little self-reflection and contemplate the wonder and power of Mother Nature. And that's exactly what I was doing while staring out the picture window of our living room at the water level that continued to rise and swallow the shoreline. But I wasn't alone. Chloe, my Aussie Shepherd, had her paws up on the windowsill, as did Captain, Josie's massive Newfie. Both of them were staring out the window, but they weren't focused on the water level. They were more interested in the dog that was sitting on our dock underneath a lamppost and staring up at the house. The dog was easy to see in the light, and it had definitely piqued both dogs' interest since their heads were cocked and they were emitting a low guttural growl.

"Sure, you're both really brave when you're inside the house," I said, laughing.

Captain glanced at me and woofed once.

"Hey, he's not bothering anybody, so let's not wake everybody else up, okay?"

Captain snorted and focused on the intruder sitting on the dock. Al and Dente, Chef Claire's Golden Retrievers, trotted into the living room looking for the reason behind the woof. I rubbed Captain's head vigorously and turned around to greet both Goldens.

"Big mouth," I said to Captain. "Did he wake you guys up?"

Al and Dente said their hellos then stretched out in front of the fireplace and went back to sleep. Moments later, Josie entered rubbing the sleep out of her eyes.

"Is everything okay? I thought I heard Captain voicing his displeasure about something."

"You did. We have a new friend down on the dock," I said, nodding out the window.

"Is that an Ibizan?" Josie said, yawning.

"Yeah," I said, then frowned. "How did you pronounce it?"

"I-*be*-zan."

"Is that the correct pronunciation? I've always said I-be-*thin*."

"That sounds more like wishful thinking," she said, grinning at me.

"Shut it."

"Or maybe you've developed a bit of a lisp."

"Geez, Josie, it's four in the morning. Don't start," I said, gently punching her on the arm.

"Not bad, huh? And I haven't even had my coffee."

"I made a pot," I said, nodding at the kitchen.

"Which leads me directly to my next question. What the heck are you doing up at four in the morning?"

"It's the first day of summer," I said, looking back out the window at the Ibizan that continued to stare at the house.

"It's going to be the first day of summer all day, Suzy."

"Yeah, I know. But I thought I might do a bit of fishing this morning."

"You didn't say anything about going fishing."

"Would you have wanted to come along?"

"Do I look like an idiot? Absolutely not," Josie said, kneeling down to rub Captain's head.

"There you go. Then there was no point mentioning it."

"Suzy, you can't go riding around in your boat in the dark with the water level this high. You've seen some of the crap floating in the River. Not to mention all the docks that are right below the surface just waiting for you to run into them."

"Hey, in case you've forgotten, I'm an expert boatswoman."

"Boatswoman?" she said, frowning. I don't think that's a word."

"Well, it oughta be," I said as I scratched Chloe's ears. "Don't worry. I've got my searchlight, and I'm going to go really slow."

"I can't believe I even have to tell you how dangerous it is out there in the dark. And it's also extremely dumb."

"It's not the dumbest thing I've ever done," I said, shrugging.

"Maybe not. But it's a lot like it. Are you taking Chloe?"

"No, it's too dan…early."

"Nice try," Josie said, shaking her head. "Just remember to take your phone in case something happens. Please, go very slow out there. And be careful you don't kill yourself." She fell silent for a moment then nodded to herself. "Okay, my work is done here. I'm going back to bed."

"Should I put the Ibizan in one of the condos?"

"Sure, if he lets you get close. If he doesn't, don't worry about it. You'll never catch him."

She turned and tossed a quick wave over her shoulder as she headed for her bedroom trailed by Captain. Chloe stretched out next to Al and Dente and fell asleep. I looked back out the window at the Ibizan who continued to look up at the house. And if I didn't know better, I would have sworn he was staring at me.

Given the fact that it was going to take me close to an hour to get where I was going, I headed for the kitchen door and managed to get out without waking the dogs. I walked down the steps, continued past the Inn, then down the front lawn. I walked across the makeshift walkway we'd set up a few weeks ago after the water had risen another six inches, and I stepped onto the edge of the floating dock.

A couple of years ago, our good friend, Rooster, had done everything he could to convince us to go with a floating dock when we had to replace our old one. Countless times over the past few months, I'd congratulated myself that we'd been smart enough to listen to him. Not only could the dock be removed in the winter thereby eliminating damage from snow and ice, but it

4

was a Godsend this year since it moved up and down with any change in the water level. Several of our friends were dealing with submerged docks at the moment, and it was making their lives miserable. And it wasn't doing much for the docks either.

I stopped on the edge of the dock and studied the Ibizan who continued to sit quietly and watch me. The *Beezer*, as the breed was commonly called, was young but not a puppy. The dog had a gorgeous brown and white coat and was lean even by Ibizan standards. I took a step forward, and it must have decided it had seen enough because it raced down the dock toward me. I froze in my tracks, then the dog launched into the air and cleared my shoulder by a foot. Stunned, I watched it sprint across our lawn, turn right, then disappear into the darkness.

"Wow," I said, dazzled by the dog's agility. "Nimble."

I untied the lines, hopped into the boat, and fired up the engine. I turned on the searchlight and slowly made my way to deeper water. As I scanned the lit area directly in front of the boat, I reviewed the long list of questions that had been bouncing around my head since I'd witnessed the event last September that precipitated my decision to be out on the River at this very moment. I hated lying to Josie, and I tried to remember if this was, in fact, the first time I had ever intentionally deceived her. I knew I'd eventually explain everything to her and she would forgive me, but telling her about my plan upfront would have been met with anger and frustration and a whole bunch of questions I couldn't answer yet.

I veered around what looked like a half-submerged kayak, and I slowed even more until I was well past a few other items that seemed to be fighting the urge to sink to the bottom of the River. Josie was right. What I was doing was incredibly stupid, but this was my one and only chance this year to see if my assumptions about her ex-boyfriend were correct. If they were, every spiritual bone in my body was about to be shattered and replaced by…

I slowed the boat even more as I pondered what they might be replaced by.

Then I realized I didn't have a clue.

I guess when everything you thought you knew gets altered or replaced, one should probably expect a sense of wonder, or at least a touch of uncertainty, to follow.

I did my best not to produce any wake as I accelerated and drove through the surreal, often frightening, darkness engulfed by a body of water that made it perfectly clear she was in charge, and I was but a tiny speck in the grand scheme of things.

Chapter 2

A white-knuckled, half-hour later, in the dim early morning light, I spotted the island I was looking for, and I anchored nearby and turned off the searchlight. I rummaged through my backpack, located my binoculars, and a container of snacks I'd brought with me. I decided I was in the mood for something salty, so I munched cashews by the handful. When I realized I'd worked my way through half the bag in ten minutes, I put them away and switched to bite-sized Snickers. After quickly devouring a half dozen, I slid the container into my backpack and chugged a bottle of water. And after chalking up my bottomless pit to nervous tension, I sat quietly and waited.

Just as the sun was beginning to peek over the horizon, I saw two shadows appear on the surface of the water about a hundred feet away. I pulled anchor and immediately began to drift toward them. They were both excited and thrashed in the water oblivious to my presence. I went back and forth about using the searchlight, then finally decided to turn it on. When the light hit both of them in the eyes, the dog barked loudly and inched closer to the man who was holding a hand up to shield his eyes. The dog's growl continued to reverberate across the water as it swam small, protective circles around the man.

"Turn that thing off," the man snapped, treading water.

"Sorry," I said, turning the searchlight off.

"Who are you?"

"It's me, Summerman. Suzy Chandler."

"Suzy? Geez, I don't believe it," the man said, shaking his head. "Should I even ask what you're doing out here?"

"Oh, I was just in the neighborhood and thought I'd stop by and say hello. Hey, Murray."

The massive dog, a Newfoundland-Golden Retriever mix that was easy to mistake for a small tiger, woofed a couple of times, then lost interest in me and swam toward the island. Summerman followed, and soon they reached shore and Summerman, naked as the day he was born, took a moment to stretch his back and limbs, and then grabbed a stick and threw it. The dog raced after it, then returned and forced Summerman into a game of tuggy. I started the boat, inched slowly toward shore, then hopped out and pulled it up on the bank of sand and rock.

I did my best to avert my eyes as Summerman glared at me. Then he nodded for me to follow him. He and the dog headed for a stone structure I knew was called the library, and I stepped inside and stood in the doorway. Murray, still holding the stick like it was a prize possession, looked up at me, and I knelt down to pet and rub his wet fur. Then he dropped the stick at my feet, and I threw it as far as I could. The dog dashed after it, and I stepped inside.

Summerman continued to glare at me as he tied his robe, then he sat down at the grand piano and started playing. He repeated

8

the same melody line several times as if committing it to memory, then he sat upright on the piano bench and shook his head at me again. Murray woofed from the other side of the screen door.

"You know how to open it," Summerman said to the dog without glancing up from the piano.

Murray softly woofed, sounding a bit miffed that he had to do it himself, but he tapped the bottom of the door with a paw, caught the partially open door with his head, then wiggled his way through. He trotted across the floor and sprawled out at Summerman's feet, staring up at him.

"Oh, I almost forgot," Summerman said, getting to his feet. "Sorry, Murray."

The dog sat up on his haunches with an expectant look on his face.

"You want a Guinness, Suzy?" Summerman said, heading for the fridge.

"No, thanks. I usually wait until the sun comes up."

Summerman shrugged and returned carrying two bottles and a dog dish. He opened both and slowly poured, then set the bowl down on the floor. We watched Murray make short work of them, then he burped and stretched back out under the piano.

"It's sort of a tradition," Summerman said by way of explanation. "Okay, we have a real problem here, and I need to know. What are you doing here?"

"Oh, I was just out doing a bit of fishing and…well, there you were."

"Suzy, we're about to have a very difficult conversation. And you lying to me is only going to make it harder."

"Okay, I came out here to look for you."

"Oh, I wish you wouldn't have done that," he said, shaking his head.

"I don't understand why it's a problem," I said.

"It's potentially a very big problem."

"For you?"

"For all of us," he said, staring hard at me. "And, yes, that most definitely includes you."

The hairs on the back of my head tingled for a moment, but I remained silent.

"Why show up today?" Summerman said.

"It's the first day of summer," I said, shrugging. "After I saw you and Murray go into the water and disappear on the last day of summer, I tried putting two and two together and figured out it was worth a shot. I thought it might clarify a few things, but now I'm more confused than ever."

"You're such a snoop."

"Yeah, I should probably start working on that."

Despite his anger, he managed a small laugh. He played the same melody line a few more times, then added to it, and it was obvious that he would much rather be playing the piano than dealing with me. But he stopped and stared off into the distance as if formulating his thoughts.

"Is that new?" I said.

"Yes. I wanted to make sure I committed it to memory. It's been rolling around my head for a while."

"For how long?"

"Nice try. If you want to go fishing, stick with the smallmouth," he said, glancing over at me.

"Point taken. But I should probably warn you, I have a lot of questions."

"I'm sure you do."

"Should I just get started?"

"Knock yourself out," he said, reaching down to rub Murray's head.

"Okay," I said, exhaling loudly. "Let's start with this one. What the hell are you?"

Summerman laughed and looked down at Murray.

"She wants to know what we are, Murray. Do you think we should tell her?"

Murray cocked his head and barked loudly once.

"That's a no," Summerman said. "In case you didn't get it."

"Do you always listen to his advice?"

"I always listen, but I don't always take it. In this case, I'm going to ignore it."

"Because you want to unburden yourself, right?"

"No, because if I don't explain a few things, you're going to drive me nuts all summer asking the same questions over and over. And that would not be a good thing."

11

Again, the hairs on the back of my neck tingled and, this time, I scratched the itch.

"What are you, Summerman?" I repeated.

"That's a really good question," he whispered, reaching down to rub the dog's head. "But for lack of a better term, I'm what's called a part-timer."

"Part-timer. But you're not talking about a category of employment," I said, raising an eyebrow.

"No, I'm not," he said, smiling. "A part-timer as in I'm only here in this form part of the year."

"Form? As in *human* form?"

"Yes."

"As weird as that sounds, Summerman, I'm gonna let that pass for the moment. Where are you the rest of the time?"

Summerman spread his arms wide and glanced up at the ceiling.

"Out there."

"I'm going to need a bit more," I said, frowning.

"Oh, you're going to need a lot more," he said, laughing. "Out there refers to the other side."

"There's another side?"

"Of course there's another side. Didn't you go to church when you were a kid?"

"Of course I did. I was raised to be a good little Catholic girl."

"Did any of it stick?"

"Funny," I said, making a face at him.

"Since you were raised Catholic, the concept of the other side must be very familiar to you."

"Sure. But it's always been a concept. Based on what I just witnessed, this is a whole lot different."

"You'll get no argument from me," Summerman said. "Isn't that right, Murray?"

The dog woofed in agreement.

"Murray's one as well?" I said.

"He certainly is."

"Part-timer?" I said, frowning. "Is that the technical term for your...situation?"

"Suzy, there's really not much about my *situation* that can be called technical. What we're looking at here falls under the category of...let's call it, unexplainable spiritual phenomena."

"Sure, sure," I said, nodding. "But there must be some physics involved, right?"

"If you're looking for a good explanation, you're not going to get it from me. I can try to explain what we go through, but I don't have a clue how it happens."

"You arrive on the first day of summer every year, and then you leave on the last day?"

"Yes," he said, softly.

"And you always come and go from the same spot in the River out front?"

"Yes."

"Why?"

13

"Probably because that's the spot where Murray and I died," Summerman said, studying my reaction.

My bottom lip quivered, and I took several short, quick breaths that seemed to echo around the room. I rediscovered my ability to breathe normally just before the onset of a panic attack.

"This is unbelievably…"

"Weird?"

"Yeah, let's go with that," I said, nodding absentmindedly as I stared off into the distance. "But it's just not possible."

"Suzy, you wouldn't believe some of the impossible things we see over there on a daily basis."

"Then maybe you better tell me a bit about the other side," I said, leaning forward.

"What do you want to know?"

"What's it like?"

"Okay, that I can tell you. Imagine having the entire universe within your grasp. And being able to go anywhere you want in the blink of an eye."

"Anywhere?"

"Sure. We can spend all day bouncing through the constellations or hovering around the beach. Or hang out here if we feel like it."

"Hovering?"

"Yeah, that's the best word I've been able to come up with to describe it."

"You'll have to excuse me if I don't believe you, Summerman," I said, sitting back in my chair.

"It doesn't matter if you believe me or not, Suzy. What matters is that you don't talk about it. To anyone. And I can't emphasize that point enough."

"Because you don't want people to think you're a nut job, right?"

"No, because I don't want Murray and me to end up as a couple of lab rats in some government experiment. And I really don't like the idea of you getting shot or your throat slit."

The look he was now giving me sent a chill up my spine. I blinked several times as he stared at me, and I felt a lump begin to form in my throat.

"So, you can actually hover anywhere you want?" I said, frowning at the absurdity of what I was asking.

"Yeah, sure. But we spend most of our time touring Earth. I always have a few things to take care of while I'm over there, and Murray likes to spend as much time near the water as he can. But we get around. Don't we, Murray?"

The dog woofed one more time and climbed out from underneath the piano. It appeared that he was following the thread of our conversation and he glanced back and forth at us as if waiting to hear what was coming next.

"I think I'm going to need a bit of proof, Summerman."

"What would you like to know?"

I pondered the question, then nodded.

"Why don't you tell me something about myself there's no way you could know," I said, pleased with the question.

"Okay, well since I left last September, you've been to the Caymans to visit your mom."

"We'd been talking about doing that for a long time. That wasn't a well-kept secret."

"No, it wasn't. But while you were down there, you and Josie rescued a group of dogs during a huge storm, decided to open another restaurant, and build an animal shelter," Summerman said, giving me a small smile. "How am I doing so far?"

"Lucky guess," I whispered.

"While you were there, two murders occurred. And, of course, you had to figure out who committed them. Nice job solving them, by the way."

"What?"

"Yeah, Bill. And his wife's name is Jerry if I remember. But then they slipped away and disappeared, right?"

"How on earth do you know that?"

"I just told you. By the way, they ended up in Cuba. I'm still trying to decide if I should tell anybody where they are. What do you think?"

"What do I think? I think something very odd is happening here," I said, stunned. "You've been spying on me?"

"No. And we don't call it spying. Do we, Murray? We were hovering. And I was keeping an eye on Josie, not you. She seems to be doing well."

16

"This isn't possible," I said, tears welling up in my eyes.

"Now do you understand why I don't want anybody to know?"

"I'm getting a headache," I said, groaning.

"Let me get you something for that," he said, getting up.

"You should probably bring the bottle."

He soon returned with a bottle of Advil and a glass of water. I downed a small handful and focused on my breathing.

"I'm having trouble accepting the fact that you can hover in anywhere you want."

"I'd be shocked if you didn't."

"Even when I'm showering?"

"That's your question? Given everything I've just told you, your biggest concern is that I might be sneaking a peek at you while you're taking a shower?"

"Well, that would be pretty creepy if you did," I said.

"Didn't you just sneak a peek at me earlier?"

"Yeah, but that was different," I said, backpedaling as fast as my little legs would go. "I was looking for you, and you just happened to be naked."

"I see."

"Checking people out while they're showering is perverted," I said, frowning.

"Yes, it is," Summerman said, nodding. "And that's why I don't do it. Unfortunately, some of the others over there aren't the gentleman I am."

"You're saying that there are dead people watching me while I shower?"

"Well, *technically*, in their current form, they aren't dead. And they certainly aren't people. But, yes, I'm sure there are."

"You're freaking me out here, Summerman."

"You asked."

"Yeah, I *really* gotta start working on that," I said, trying to catch my breath.

"It's a little late for that, don't you think?" Summerman said, casually as he lit a cigarette.

"I didn't know you smoked," I said.

"Only occasionally," he said, exhaling smoke. "Usually when I'm stressed. And I think this qualifies."

"Don't you know those things will kill you?" I said, then shook my head when I realized the stupidity of my comment.

"I'll take my chances," he said, chuckling. "By the way, your Dad said to say hi."

My eyes grew wide, then tears began to stream down my cheeks. Summerman headed into the kitchen and returned with a box of tissues. I grabbed a handful and tried to stem the flow.

"That was an incredibly cruel thing to say, Summerman."

"I'm sorry," Summerman said. "That wasn't my intention. I was just passing along his message."

"I should have stayed in bed," I said, sobbing.

"Without a doubt. But you didn't, and now we need to deal with it."

"My father really said that?"

"No, I just made it up to see if I could make you bawl like a baby," he said, shaking his head. "Of course, he said it. And if he's around at the moment, I'm sure he's also wondering what the heck you're doing here."

"What do you mean if he's around?" I said, glancing around the library.

"I always attract quite a crowd on crossover day," Summerman said, running his fingers over the keyboard. "For some reason, most people over there get a kick out of watching us arrive. But I think most of them are just envious. Go ahead and give them a little wave. That always breaks them up."

"I think I'm going to throw up."

And then I did. All over the tile floor. Murray scurried back under the piano for cover while Summerman headed off to grab some towels. He handed me one, and I wiped my mouth and clothes while he cleaned up the mess I'd made on the floor.

"You probably shouldn't eat candy this early in the morning," he said, glancing over his shoulder.

"It wasn't the candy," I snapped, then stretched out on a couch. "I'm so sorry."

"Don't worry about it," he said, climbing to his feet holding two of the used towels at arm's length. "Considering what you've just learned, vomiting is the least of your problems."

"You really see my father over there?" I said, working myself into a sitting position.

He tossed the towels aside, then sat on the floor with his back against the couch.

"Sure. He tends to hang around the River most of the time, so I usually see him whenever I'm in the area."

"He spends his time around here?"

"Yes. He likes to keep a close eye on you and your mom."

"And you talk to each other?"

"Well, we certainly communicate. But it's not really talking. It's more of an innate understanding. Everybody just seems to know what others are thinking."

"So, it's what, telepathic?"

"I don't know what it is," Summerman said, shaking his head. "But it's pretty cool. As long as you don't mind knowing what everybody truly thinks about you."

"I think I'm going to throw up again," I said, lurching forward.

And then I did. All over Summerman. He grimaced when some of the vomit landed on the back of his head and dripped down his robe. He handled the situation with a lot more grace and dignity than I would have, and he grabbed the used towels and wiped up the new mess I'd made. Then he climbed to his feet and looked at me.

"I need to shower," he said, giving me what I was sure was a forced smile. "Are you going to be okay alone for a few minutes?"

"I'm fine," I said, getting to my feet. "Look, I should get going."

"Suzy, we haven't finished our conversation," he said, his voice rising.

"I know," I said, wobbling slightly. I put my hand on the couch for support and focused on my breathing. "But I think this is all I can handle for now."

"Okay," he said, softly. "But not a word, Suzy. To anyone. And that includes Josie."

"She needs to know, Summerman."

"Yes, she does. But I'm going to be the one to tell her. Do you understand?"

I managed a nod, then had another thought.

"How many people know about your situation?"

"On this side?"

"Well, I imagine that pretty much everybody on the other side knows, right?"

"Now you're going to get snarky with me?" he said, raising an eyebrow at me.

"Sorry," I said, rubbing my forehead. "I'm a bit overloaded at the moment. Yes, I'm talking about on this side."

"Counting you, four. Josie will make it five. And it stops there. Do you understand what I'm telling you, Suzy?"

"I got it," I snapped. "Geez, you're starting to sound like my mother."

"It's so nice to be back," he said, shaking his head. "We'll need to continue this conversation soon."

"Sure, sure. Why don't you swing by the restaurant tonight?"

"Maybe I'll do that," he said. "How is she doing?"

"She's great," I said. "Everything is really good at the moment. Apart from the water level, of course. And nobody has been killed in six months, so that's good, right?"

"I'm afraid that's about to change," Summerman whispered.

"What are you talking about?" I said as my Snoopmeter turned itself on. "Somebody's about to get killed?"

"Yeah, I think so. If it hasn't happened already."

"Summerman, I don't think I can process any more revelations today, so let's just cut to the chase, okay?"

"I don't know much about it," he said, shrugging. "Somebody on the other side asked me to keep an eye on someone who recently came back to the area. People are always asking me to do favors for them while I'm over here. And I'd been pretty busy over there, but a couple of days ago I had a few minutes to spare, so we hovered in to see what was going on."

"What did you find out?"

"Nothing. But like I said, I only had a few minutes, and when he wasn't where the person said he was going to be, we moved on."

"Who is it?" I said, gently rubbing my stomach that continued to rumble.

"I don't even know," he said. "I had no idea who the person who asked was, and I didn't pay very close attention to what she was saying. Like I said, people are always asking me to do favors for them, and there's no way I can get to all of them. I told her I'd

22

take a look, but I was in a hurry and should have listened more carefully."

"That's all the information you have? Some unknown person is about to get killed?"

"Or already has," Summerman said. "All I remember from the conversation is that it was a guy in his late forties who always wore a baseball cap of a minor league team."

"Do you remember which team it was?"

"Sure," he said, laughing. "The team's name is impossible to forget. The Normal CornBelters."

"Odd name," I said. "Where are they located?"

"I have no idea. But if it were me, I'd probably start the search by looking somewhere in the Midwest," he deadpanned. "You know, Corn Country."

"Good thinking," I said, making a face at him. "Do you remember anything else?"

"Yeah, apparently he has a dog that goes everywhere with him."

"What kind of dog?"

"I don't know the breed. But it's supposed to be really fast and a great jumper."

"Wow."

"What is it?"

"I think I might have seen the dog this morning. It was sitting on my dock."

My neurons overloaded as my stress level collided with my Snoopmeter that was redlining. I stared out at the River overwhelmed by the morning's events.

"Maybe he'll come back. What kind of dog was it?" he said, watching me closely. "Are you okay, Suzy?"

"I-be-thin," I blurted.

He gave me a puzzled look and held his stare.

"Your rather bizarre transition into urban slang aside, I agree. You look great."

Chapter 3

I staggered outside to my boat. Summerman and Murray followed me to make sure I could get the bow off the shore and back into the water. As we approached the boat, I reached out and poked a finger into Summerman's shoulder. He stared at me like I'd lost my mind, which could have very well been the case, and I felt my face flush red with embarrassment. I forced a smile and shrugged at him.

"Sorry. Just checking," I said, giving the bow a push.

"What did you expect? A misty vapor? Again, do not say a word to anyone, Suzy," he said with purpose.

I nodded and climbed into the boat and fired up the engine. I backed away from shore and gave him a small wave as I pointed the boat downriver. He walked toward the library rubbing the back of his neck vigorously, then he wiped his hand on his robe.

The sun was up, and it looked like it was going to be a nice day. It had to get better from here, I decided, and I reviewed the events of the past hour and tried to comprehend what I'd seen and what Summerman had told me.

A dead person who comes back to life three months out of the year?

It was a ridiculous idea, and the sort of nonsense mental institutions must be filled with. But I'd seen it with my own eyes, and there was no way I could explain how he and his dog magically appeared in the River out of thin air. I was also at a loss when it came to how he knew the details of our activities in the Caymans. I felt my stomach flip and roll again, and I slowed to a crawl as I stared out at the water.

I entered a narrower section of the River near the shore of the mainland and noticed another boat heading in my direction. I snapped out of my funk momentarily and veered right as I accelerated to give the other boat room to pass and the right of way. I waved to the other boater as she passed, then slipped back inside my head to ponder Summerman, the guy in the baseball hat who was apparently about to be killed, and my place in the universe in general. I continued to let my mind race and wander until I was brought back to reality in the blink of an eye.

I hit the submerged dock hard, but not hard enough to throw me overboard to a watery grave, and I felt the bottom of my boat scrape against wood as it slowed. Then I heard the unmistakable sound of my outboard engine's lower unit being sheared off. The boat stopped with the bow tilted downward in the water with the stern perched on the submerged dock. The engine continued to run, but without a propeller, I knew I wasn't going far. I turned off the motor and peered over the stern to examine the damage. The motor was toast, but at least the boat wasn't taking on water.

I forced myself to focus, took a moment to thank my lucky stars, and grabbed my phone. I dialed the number and waited for the call to connect.

"Hey, Suzy. You're up early."

"Hi, Rooster. I've been up for hours. Look, I hate to bother you, but I need your help."

"Sure, what's up?"

"I'm stuck."

"Oh, are you doing the Times's crossword? For the life of me, I cannot figure out 37 across."

"I'm stuck out on the River, Rooster."

"Okay. I'm probably going to need a bit more," he said, turning serious.

"I just ran into the McMaster's dock and tore my lower unit off."

"Are you hurt?"

"No, just my pride as someone who's supposed to know her way around the River."

"Are you taking on water?"

"No, the boat's fine. But I'm gonna need a tow."

"I'm on my way."

"Thanks, Rooster," I said, hanging up.

I slipped the phone back into my pocket then gently bounced up and down on the tip of my toes. It was pretty clear that the boat wasn't going anywhere. I was about to sit while I waited and see if I could manage to keep a snack down when I heard a woman's voice coming from shore.

"Are you okay?"

I waved to the elderly woman I'd known since I was a little girl. And she and her two Dobermans were long-standing customers at the Inn. The dogs stood on either side of her and had their heads cocked as if they couldn't believe what they were seeing.

"Hi, Mrs. McMaster. Yes, I'm fine. But I think I did some damage to your dock. Don't worry, I'll pay to get it fixed."

"Is that you, Suzy?"

"Yeah, it's me," I said. "I'm so sorry. I never saw it."

"Don't worry about it. The dock can be fixed," she said, folding her arms across her chest. "I'm just glad you weren't hurt."

"Luckily, I wasn't going very fast," I said, then for some reason felt the need to offer her a bit of sage advice. "You know, Mrs. McMaster, most folks are putting out markers to let others know there's something just below the surface."

The elderly woman shook her head at me and pointed out at the water. I turned around and saw, for the first time, two large, bright blue barrels that were sitting on the end of the dock.

"Sure, sure," I said, embarrassed. "I never even saw them. Again, I'm so sorry, Mrs. McMaster."

"Accidents happen, dear. Do you need me to call someone?"

"No, Rooster is on his way. Thanks."

"Okay, then," she said. "I have something on the stove I need to tend to. Say hi to your mom for me. And you and Josie should stop by sometime."

"We'll do that, Mrs. McMaster," I said, waving.

"And maybe you should just drive your car when you do come for a visit," she said, chuckling as she waved and headed back up the hill to her house.

"Everybody's a comedian," I said to myself as I rummaged through the container of snacks.

I was just about to tear open one of the bite-sized when I saw Rooster's work boat heading toward me. I popped the Snickers into my mouth and waved. His German Shepherd, Titan, was sitting in the seat next to him keeping a close eye on all the action. Moments later, he slowed the boat and put it in neutral. He drifted closer keeping a close eye on the submerged dock. Rooster grabbed my stern and glanced around at the damage.

"Nice job," he said, shaking his head.

"Yeah, not one of my finer moments. I wasn't paying attention."

"Do I even need to tell you how lucky you are?"

"Oh, I wish you wouldn't," I said.

"Suzy, you need to be careful out here until the water level drops," he said. "The entire River landscape is very different from what we're used to."

"I know that," I snapped. "I just got a little distracted."

"Geez, okay," he said, showing me his palms in mock surrender. "I know you're a bit rattled, but let's dial it down a notch. What are you doing out here this early in the morning anyway?"

"I was fishing."

"Where's your fishing gear?" he said, glancing around my boat.

"It must have gone overboard in the crash," I said, staring out at the water.

"Okay, have it your way," he said, grabbing a piece of rope. "Attach this to the bow."

I took one end of the rope and secured it, then headed to the stern. Rooster tied the other end of the rope to the back of his boat and gestured for me to climb aboard. I tossed the snack container to him, then stood on the side of my boat and stepped toward his. I made it halfway, slipped, then fell forward onto the deck of his boat. I picked myself up and checked for damage. Apart from a skinned elbow and a severely bruised ego, I decided I was fine.

"Smooth," Rooster said, grinning. "Very ladylike."

"Shut it," I said, glaring at him, then I knelt down to pet the dog. "How are you doing, Titan?"

Rooster slowly maneuvered his boat until the tow rope was tight, then he slowly accelerated. My boat groaned a bit as it scraped along the dock and then the stern softly splashed as it reentered the water. We took a moment to make sure the boat wasn't leaking, then Rooster headed toward his place of business where he operated a small marina during the summer and an engine repair shop the remainder of the year.

"Are you okay?" he said, glancing over.

"I'm fine. Why do you ask?"

"Because you look like you've seen a ghost."

"Yeah?" I said, staring out at the River. "Maybe I should take a selfie for posterity."

"What?"

"Nothing. I'm just babbling."

"You're acting a little weird today, Suzy. Even by your standards."

"It's been an eventful morning."

"Well, running into a dock like that will certainly get your attention."

"What's that? Oh, yeah. The dock. Sure, sure."

"You didn't hit your head did you?"

"No, I just threw up a couple of times."

Chapter 4

After we got my boat back to Rooster's and I'd placed the order for a new motor, he dropped me off at the Inn. I headed inside and was greeted near the front door by Chloe and Bailey, the bloodhound we'd rescued in the Cayman Islands. Josie was chatting with Sammy and Jill at the reception desk, and they all seemed a bit taken aback when they saw the look on my face.

"What did you do, swim home?" Josie said.

"What?" I said, still trying to clear my head.

"Where's the boat?"

"Oh, I ran into a dock," I said, heading for my office.

"You did what?" Josie said, following me.

I sat down behind my desk and tried to ignore the stare she was giving me. I opened my laptop and was about to start typing when she gently closed the monitor on my fingers.

"I can't see the screen," I said, glancing up at her. "Move your hand. Please."

"I believe you said something about running into a dock?" she said, raising an eyebrow.

"Oh, that. Yeah, Mrs. McMaster's. She said to say hi and that we should stop by sometime."

"You ran into a dock in the middle of the night," she said, scolding me with a shake of her head. "What did I tell you about going out there in the dark?"

"It wasn't the middle of the night. There was plenty of light. I just didn't see it," I said, opening the laptop again.

"Well, then I guess that makes all the difference," she said. "What are you doing?"

"I'm looking for the Normal CornBelters," I said, typing.

"As opposed to the abnormal ones?"

"I suppose," I said, focusing on the search results. "Oh, by the way, we're going to C's tonight. And I told Summerman to stop by."

"Summerman? My Summerman?"

"How many do you know?" I said, clicking on one of the links. "How about that? Did you know there's actually a town called Normal?"

"When did you see Summerman?" Josie said, continuing to stare at me in disbelief.

"There they are. The Normal CornBelters. Normal, Illinois. It's right outside Bloomington. I thought Bloomington was in Indiana. There must be more than one. Huh. I wonder if everybody who lives there really is normal. Whatever the heck normal is, right?"

"Suzy?" Josie whispered.

"Yeah?"

"Are you sure you're okay?"

"I'm fine," I said, reading from the screen.

"You didn't hit your head, did you?"

"No, I just threw up a couple of times."

"You threw up twice?"

"Yeah, but only once on Summerman."

Josie reached forward, closed the laptop again, then sat down and studied me closely.

"Where did you run into Summerman?"

"I didn't run into him. I ran into a dock."

"Okay," she said, frowning. "Then where did you *see* him?"

"At his island."

"That's where you went this morning?" she said, frowning.

"Yeah," I said, glancing at her as tears formed in my eyes.

"Why are you crying?" she said, giving me a wild-eyed stare. "What on earth did he say to you?"

"Oh, I'm sure he'll tell you all about it tonight."

"I really wish you'd tell me now," she said, then sat back in her chair, obviously concerned with my well-being. "Okay, I can wait."

"But you might want to hold off eating dinner until after you've chatted."

"Suzy, why don't you head up to the house and go back to bed for a while?"

"Okay, that sounds like a good idea."

I got up and left the office and walked up the path to the house in a daze. Halfway up, I crossed paths with Chef Claire who was

34

on her way to work. She beamed at me, then stopped when she saw the look on my face.

"Good morning," she said. "Are you all right?"

"Yeah, why?"

"You look like you've seen a ghost," she said.

"I'm fine. Oh, Josie and I will be stopping by for dinner tonight," I said, staring off into the distance.

"Okay," she said, frowning. "Then I guess I'll see you later."

"Sure, sure," I said as I watched her head to her car.

I removed my phone and held it out in front of me to take a selfie. Since people were fond of using the expression *you look like you've just seen a ghost*, I thought it would be a good idea to have a picture of exactly what it looked like just in case I ever needed to refer to it.

Or be reminded.

Chapter 5

I napped on and off for a couple of hours and dreamt of red-eyed spectral visions lurking around every corner who were just waiting for me to flash a bit of skin. The last one must have been a nightmare because I woke up drenched in sweat, mummy-wrapped in my sheets and blanket. I extricated myself and headed for the bathroom. I tossed my soaked pajamas and sheets in the hamper, glanced around the bathroom for signs of hoverers, then slowly opened the shower door and peered inside.

I spent the next few minutes trying to lather up and cover myself at the same time, then realized I was being ridiculous. I was less certain but still worried about the very real possibility that I'd lost the plot completely and was destined to spend my remaining days wandering the streets with a nervous twitch and permanent vacant stare. And it was only after I remembered that I'd be way down the list of likely candidates for any Peeping Tom spirits searching for titillation that I was finally able to relax and enjoy the rest of my shower.

As soon as I'd slipped into my robe and my thoughts coalesced on the mysterious man in the baseball hat, I began to feel a bit better. I put Summerman away in my *to be dealt with later* file, turned on my hair dryer, then immediately turned it off when a light bulb went off. I pulled on a pair of jeans and a tee shirt and headed down to the Inn.

I came in the back door, and instead of making my usuals rounds of saying good morning to all the dogs, I headed straight for the reception area. Sammy was on the phone, and I did my best to wait patiently for him to finish. As he listened to what the person on the other end of the call was saying, he glanced at my wet hair then down at my bare feet. He nestled the phone under his chin and tapped the keyboard in front of him.

"You're all set, Betty. Tuesday at eleven. We'll see you then," he said, hanging up the phone. Then he stared at me and deadpanned, "I'm sorry, ma'am. But our policy is no shoes, no service."

"Funny," I said, flashing him a fake grin. "I have a question."

"You're dripping on the floor, Suzy."

"Forget the dripping," I said, glancing down at the small puddle forming around my feet. "Didn't you tell me one time that you spent a year going to college in Bloomington?"

"Yeah, I did," he said. "But not the Bloomington in Indiana where IU is. The one in Illinois. I went to a small state school there."

"That's great."

"The people at IU would probably disagree with you, but why do you ask?"

"Remind me again, how did you end up there?"

"It was right around the time when my folks were splitting up, and I was having a hard time dealing with it. I had some family in Illinois, and they offered to put me up if I wanted to go to school out there. But I missed being here and only lasted a year before I transferred out."

"You've got family in Bloomington?"

"Yeah, my dad's brother lives there. At least he did. I'm not sure where he is now. He hit a rough patch and, from what I hear from my cousin, he basically disappeared."

"Really?" I said, staring off into the distance. "No, it couldn't be, could it?"

If the wall I was talking to knew the answer, it didn't say. Sammy continued to stare at me, then he nodded at Josie who was walking by. Josie approached and gave me the once over.

"I thought you were going to take a nap," she said, grabbing a strand of my wet hair. "But I see you opted for an incomplete shower. Good call."

"I finished showering," I said, glancing over at her. "I just didn't finish drying."

"Why do you care about my time in Illinois?" Sammy said, thoroughly confused.

"I'm trying to find out some things about a minor league baseball team that's located there," I said.

"There's no team in Bloomington," Sammy said.

"There's not?" I said, frowning.

"No, technically it's right next door in Normal."

"The CornBelters?"

"Yeah, the Normal CornBelters. How'd you know that? Great name, huh? The CornBelters. And they play their games in a stadium called the Corn Crib," he said, grinning at Josie. "Get it?"

"Yeah, I'm sensing a theme here," Josie said, then turned to me. "Okay, Snoopmeister, you've got that look. Why the sudden interest in some obscure baseball team?"

I started to respond but stopped when I wondered how I could explain it without revealing where I'd gotten the information. More importantly, I didn't want to say anything that might reveal too much about Summerman's situation. Unable to carve out a path, I decided to go for a generality.

"Oh, I just heard that someone was wearing a baseball hat with that name on it and thought it was clever. I was thinking about maybe getting one. You know how I am about hats. And then I remembered that Sammy had spent some time in Illinois."

"Yeah, okay," Josie said, giving me a look that told me in no uncertain terms she knew I was either lying, hiding something or probably both.

"So, you're familiar with the team?" I said to Sammy.

"Sure, my cousin and his dad and I used to go to games all the time the summer I was there," Sammy said. "In fact, my cousin actually *plays* for them now."

Stunned, I stared at him, then again looked off into the distance as several light bulbs popped in my head. A family of baseball fans, a father who disappeared, the son who ended up playing for the team in question, a man in danger of being killed who loved wearing the team hat, and a member of the family who worked for us was standing three feet away.

I decided that it being merely a series of coincidences was about as likely as me spending the morning with a real-life ghost. Deciding that it must be a day for miracles, I glanced at Sammy who continued to look at me with genuine concern.

"Was your cousin's father a dog lover?" I said.

"Oh, yeah. He was a huge dog guy," Sammy said, nodding. "And he loved this one breed in particular. But I can never remember the name."

Josie stared at me in disbelief, and I nodded.

"Ibizan?" I whispered.

"That's it," Sammy said. "How the heck did you know that?"

"I guess I'm just in touch with the universe today," I said, exhaling loudly.

Chapter 6

I pulled into one of our assigned parking spots in the back of the restaurant and turned the car off. I glanced over at Josie who was understandably nervous about seeing Summerman, and I patted her forearm. She flinched, then looked over at me like she'd forgotten I was there, then forced a smile.

"This is going to be really strange," she said.

"You have no idea," I said, opening my door.

"What?"

"Nothing. But don't worry, everything is going to be fine. And you look fantastic."

It was true. She did. And she ought to look great since it had taken her almost two hours to get ready. It was almost eight o'clock, well past my dinner hour, and I was anxious to get inside. I took the return of my appetite as a sign that I was well on my way to a full recovery, and I was more than ready to test my theory. I was also in a hurry for her to have the conversation with Summerman so I'd have some help trying to process the unbelievable news I'd received that morning.

"I think I went overboard with this blouse," she said, climbing out of the car. "Is it too much?"

"Only for the men with bad hearts," I said, locking the car. "C'mon, I know exactly what I'm having."

She stood by the car and took several deep breaths. I frowned impatiently but gave her all the time she needed. She and Summerman had fallen madly in love last summer, but after he had told her that he could only see her three months out of the year, things had quickly fallen apart. At the time, neither one of us could understand why he couldn't be around for at least some of the other nine months of the year, and he'd been very evasive about the reason why. Now that I knew the answer, it made perfect sense, or as much sense as anything else about his situation did, and I was extremely interested in seeing how she would respond when she heard the news.

We headed inside C's through the kitchen door and waved at Chef Claire who was dealing with a long line of order slips. She gave us a quick wave, then refocused on the task at hand, and barked at a couple of her servers. Normally the sweetest person in the world, she turned into a growling four-star general whenever she was working her magic in the kitchen. We made our way through the kitchen and into the bar that was jam-packed.

I heard a familiar melody and glanced over at the piano sitting in the far corner. The piece of music had changed dramatically since I'd first heard it this morning, and Summerman, oblivious to everyone else in the room, had his head down as his fingers effortlessly ran up and down the keyboard. Murray was draped across his feet underneath the piano.

We elbowed our way into a small space at the bar, and I waved to Rocco, our head bartender. He nodded at me and went back to work filling a large drink order for Wendy, a college student who was working for us this summer as a waitress. She gave us a smile and a wave and listened to Summerman while she waited for her drinks.

"Where the heck did all these people come from?" I said to her.

"It's pretty amazing," Wendy said. "A half-hour ago, there might have been ten people in the bar. Then he walked in and just started playing. Somebody must have sent out a text or something because it started filling up five minutes later. Who is that guy?"

"That's Summerman Lawless," I said.

"No way," Wendy said. "That's him? I heard he had a place around here. But I thought he was a rocker. That sounds a lot like jazz."

"He can play anything," Josie said, staring at the piano player.

"Here you go, Wendy," Rocco said, sliding the tray of drinks closer to her.

"Thanks, Rocco," she said, carefully lifting the tray and heading back into the dining room.

"How are you guys doing tonight?" Rocco said, turning to us.

"We're good," I said, nodding. "Busy, huh?"

"Yeah, you should hire that guy for the summer," he said, laughing. "His rate can't be more than fifty, sixty thousand a night, right? What can I get you?"

"I'll have a glass of that nice Sauvignon from New Zealand," I said, then glanced at Josie who nodded. "Two of those, please."

Summerman continued to put on a dazzling display, then he slowed down, and I heard the exact melody line I'd listened to this morning. I closed my eyes, let the gentle phrase wash over me, and I was transported back to earlier in the day. I felt my stomach begin to toss and turn and was grateful when Summerman finished to wild applause. He thanked the crowd then looked around and spotted us at the bar. He headed straight for us, trailed by Murray. The dog only got a few steps before he stopped to enjoy the attention he was getting from several people. But Summerman made his way to the bar undeterred. He stopped directly in front of Josie, and they stared into each other's eyes for a long time.

I waited it out, killing time by gulping down half of my wine and munching on peanuts.

"How are you?" Summerman said to Josie.

"I'm good. It's nice to see you."

"Hi, Suzy," Summerman said. "Long time, no see."

"Hey, Summerman. Glad you could make it."

"I wouldn't have missed it," he said, turning to Josie. "Can we talk? There's something I need to explain to you."

"Sure, go ahead," she said.

He cleared his throat, glanced around the crowd, then nodded at the door.

"We should probably do it outside. It's pretty loud in here. Can we go for a walk?"

"I guess that would be okay," she said, setting her wine glass down on the bar.

"Should I order you guys some dinner?" I said.

"No, you better wait until we get back," Summerman said. "This could take some time."

"Got it," I said. "But I need to eat."

"Go ahead," Josie said.

"Try not to freak out," I said, smiling at her.

"What's the matter with you?" she said.

"Nothing's the matter. Why do you ask?" I said, frowning.

"I was just expecting a few snarky comments. Like the one about how you hope I'd be able to keep my clothes on until we get out of the restaurant. Or something along those lines."

"Maybe later," I whispered with a shrug. "Let's see how this plays out first."

"You're kind of freaking me out today, Suzy," she said, taking Summerman's hand.

"Yeah, *I'm* the problem," I whispered into my wine glass.

"What?"

"Nothing. You two have fun."

She studied my face, tried to make some sense of what I was saying, then gave up, and followed Summerman. I watched them wiggle their way through the throng until they went out the front door. I glanced around the crowded bar looking for potential dinner companions. While I didn't mind eating alone, I was in the mood for company tonight. I eventually spotted my mother with

Chief Abrams and Freddie, our local medical examiner, sitting on a couch near the fireplace and I made my way over to them.

"Darling," my mother said. "What a nice surprise. I thought you were going to spend the evening home."

"Slight change of plans," I said, leaning over to buss her cheek.

"Can I ask you what you were doing out on the River in the middle of the night?" she said.

"Word travels fast. I was fishing."

"I see. Can I ask you why?"

"Well, I can't really catch anything sitting in my living room," I snapped.

"Okay, darling, let's not do this here," she said, scowling.

"And it wasn't the middle of the night," I said, surprised by my own petulance. "Chief, Freddie, how are you guys doing?"

"Well, nobody died today, so I'm good," Freddie said, shrugging. "And it's been so quiet lately, I'm starting to feel bad taking your money, Mrs. C."

My mother, the mayor of Clay Bay, considered his comment as she took a sip of wine. "You can always give it back, Freddie. And for the record, it's not my money. If it were, you'd be looking at a major pay cut."

"Touché," Chief Abrams said, laughing. "We were just heading in for dinner. Would you like to join us?"

"You read my mind, Chief."

"Oh, for his sake, let's hope not," my mother said, laughing. "That's a place where even angels fear to tread."

Chief Abrams and Freddie roared with laughter, and I glared at her.

"You're really not funny, Mom."

"Oh, I disagree, darling."

Chapter 7

I studied the menu. I had no idea why since I'd had my order ready since early this morning. I ordered a ribeye with a side of mushrooms, but instead of my usual baked potato, I went with one of Chef Claire's latest creations. She had been experimenting with some recipes for our new restaurant in the Caymans when she hit on the idea of slicing potatoes lengthwise into paper-thin slices and then stuffing them with a variety of fillings and rolling them tight. Then she fried them in peanut oil until golden brown, but they remained incredibly soft in the middle. They were like gourmet stuffed French fries and were already a major hit. I couldn't decide which filling to go with, so I went with a sampling of all four varieties. I listened to Chief Abrams order the exact same thing and glanced over at him.

"Copycat," I said, clinking glasses with him.

"You've never steered me wrong before," he said. "How was your day?"

"Memorable is a word that comes to mind," I said, taking a big gulp of Sauvignon.

"You gonna share?"

"For now, just a little of it," I said, glancing around the crowded dining room. "Have you seen anybody walking around wearing a baseball hat with a funny looking logo?"

"Dozens of them. All the time."

"Yeah, I imagine a bit more specificity might help, huh? This one has a cartoon face of an ear of corn with eyes. The name of the team is the Normal CornBelters. They're a minor league team in Illinois."

"No, it doesn't ring a bell," he said, pausing with his wine glass near his mouth to give it some thought. "Cool name though. What's the deal with the guy in the hat?"

"I heard a rumor that the guy might be in danger," I whispered.

"A rumor? I see," he said, studying my face. "Can I ask where you heard it?"

"Oh, I really wish you wouldn't," I said, giving him a small smile.

"Okay," he said, nodding slowly. "I guess that can wait for now. What sort of danger is he supposed to be in?"

"Somebody plans on killing him, or maybe already has," I whispered as I reached for the bread basket.

"And that's all you know? It's not much to go on, Suzy," Chief Abrams said, waving the bread basket away.

I launched into my summary of all the various bits of information I'd learned today, with the notable exception of everything related to Summerman. When I finished, I sat back in my chair and waited for him to respond.

"And Sammy might be related to the guy in the hat?"

"Yeah. I'm almost positive he is," I said, sitting back in my chair to give our waiter room to refill our wine glasses.

"And it's the same dog breed?" he said, puzzled.

"Yes. So, what do you think?"

"I'm going to have to agree with you. That's a whole lot of coincidences."

"What are you going to do?" I said.

"What do you mean?" he said, frowning.

"Well, we need to track him down, don't we? You know, before something bad happens to him."

"Suzy, I can pass the word around to some of my colleagues in the area, but it's not like I can just put out an APB on a guy just because he's wearing a corn hat."

"Why not?"

"Well, for one, because I don't want to look like an idiot. And all I have is some vague rumor about how he might be in danger. But if you want to go into some of the specifics about the source of the rumor, my answer might be different," he said, grinning at me with a raised eyebrow.

"Nice try, Chief."

"Okay, your call. Suzy, even if we do find him, all I can do is warn him, and ask him if he's aware he might be in danger. There wouldn't be anything to hold him on."

"Unless he asked for protection, right?"

"Yeah, if he asked for it, we might be able to do something. But if he's concerned about his wellbeing and does want some help from the police, don't you think we would have already heard from him by now?"

"Geez, Chief," I said, laughing. "If you're going to use logic, what chance do I have to convince you?"

"Yeah, those dang pesky facts will get you every time. They're always getting in the way and messing things up. But I will get the word out and keep my eyes open. If we do find the dog, I'll bring him by the Inn."

"I doubt if you'll be able to catch him," I said, building a small plate from the antipasto that had been placed in the center of the table. "Beezers can run like a deer and are great jumpers. This morning, the dog sailed right over my shoulder without breaking a sweat."

"I'm not familiar with the breed," Chief Abrams said, also helping himself to the antipasto.

"They're great dogs. Really smart, and terrific with people once they're socialized. But they can be very sensitive, especially when their routine gets disrupted or if they get stressed."

"And the way the dog ran away from you this morning makes you think something might have already happened to his owner? This mysterious guy in the corn hat."

"Now that I hear you say it out loud, it does sound like I might be overreaching on this one," I said, frowning.

"Maybe," he said, shrugging as he nibbled on a piece of cheese. "But you've had weirder ideas before that turned out to be right."

"But why would the dog show up on our dock?" I said, frowning.

"Why are you asking me?" Chief Abrams said. "You're the dog guru."

"Darling, if I didn't know better, I'd swear you were ignoring me. What on earth are you two talking about?"

"Sorry, Mom. I'm just trying to make sense of a few things that happened today."

"Try to not force it," she said, glancing around the table. "You're always in such a hurry to get all the answers. Give it some time. I've always found that I always feel better when I relax and let things reveal themselves."

"Revelation sure didn't make me feel any better this morning," I whispered.

Chief Abrams heard my comment and gave me an odd look. I glanced over at him, then noticed that my mom and Freddie were also studying me closely.

"Yeah, that's probably good advice," I said.

I was about to reach for another piece of bread when I noticed Josie slowly making her way to the table. She was walking unsteadily, and her face was drawn tight and drained of color. She placed a hand on the back of my chair in an attempt to steady herself and remained standing.

"Hello, dear," my mother said. "Where's Summerman?"

"Uh, he had to leave," she said to my mother without making eye contact.

"Are you okay, Josie?" my mother said. "You look like you've seen a ghost."

Josie managed a soft chuckle, then she exhaled audibly.

"Have a seat," Freddie said, sliding the chair next to him back a bit.

"No, I don't think I can stay for dinner," she said.

"Why not?" Freddie said.

"Please, join us, dear," my mother said, gesturing at the empty chair.

"No, thanks. I'm not hungry."

Freddie and Chief Abrams both laughed, but my mother stared at Josie with a look of genuine concern.

"Are you okay?"

"No, I'm really not feeling well," Josie said, then touched my shoulder. "Would you mind taking me home?"

"Sure, no problem," I said, getting up from my chair. "Let's go. I'm sorry to cut out early, Mom."

"Don't worry about it," she said, continuing to watch Josie closely. "I hope you feel better, dear."

"Could you just have my dinner boxed up and sent home with Chef Claire?" I said to my mother. I looked up at Josie and patted her hand to get her attention. "You sure you don't want to order something for later?"

"No, I'm fine," Josie said, giving the table a small wave as she headed for the door.

I followed her outside, helped her into the car, then we drove home in silence. We both changed into comfortable clothes, then I made a pot of coffee, and we settled down in the living room surrounded by the dogs who were delighted to see us. Josie rubbed Captain's head and continued to stare out the picture window in a state of shock. I had a pretty good feel for what she was going through, so I stayed quiet as long as I could. Even though I was still at a loss for words to describe what we'd both learned today, I eventually I broke the silence.

"Weird, huh?" I said.

"Yeah, that's a word for it," she said, then gave me a small smile. "That's the best you got? Weird?"

"Well, I suppose I could string a bunch of adjectives to it, but they'd probably all be of the four-letter variety."

"How is this possible?"

"I have no idea," I said, shaking my head. "You believe him, right?"

"How could I not? He told me things that nobody else knows."

"Yeah, he did the same thing with me. He started talking about my dad."

"He told me how bad he felt when he watched me bawl my eyes out for two weeks last year after he left," Josie said.

"I didn't know you did that," I said, genuinely surprised by the news. "I had no idea."

"Nobody knows," she said. "And that's what convinced me he was telling the truth."

"You know, once I got past the shock, I started thinking about how cool it would be to go back and forth like that," I said.

"He thinks he might keep doing it forever," she said.

"Eternal? Even better, right?" I said, shrugging. "Did he talk about what it's like on the other side?"

"A little. Then I started crying and asked him to go home."

"It's a lot to deal with. I've been walking around in a daze all day," I said.

"I noticed. And now I understand why," she said, grudgingly relinquishing a portion of the couch as Captain stretched out. "We really need to get you on a diet."

"How could you say something that cruel?"

"I was talking to the dog," she said, laughing.

"Oh," I said, relaxing. "So, what are you going to do?"

"About Summerman? I have no idea. But I'll probably start by keeping my distance from him for a while."

"That's going to be hard to do."

"It certainly is," she said.

"I think this is definitely the strangest day I've ever experienced. And I could use a distraction. You feel like watching a movie?" I said, reaching for the remote.

"Sure. Anything to take my mind off this subject."

I started scrolling through the selection of movies. Then I paused and looked over at her.

"You know what bothers me the most?"

"Knowing you, it's probably the idea that there's a bunch of spirits on the other side who can see you naked."

"Lucky guess," I said, embarrassed. "I actually tried covering myself up when I took a shower today."

"That must make it a bit hard to get at all the nooks and crannies," she deadpanned. Then she had a thought and frowned. "Suzy, please tell me you aren't going to start showering in your bathing suit."

"I have to admit that the thought did cross my mind."

"We really need to find you a boyfriend," she said, shaking her head.

We both turned around when we heard the kitchen door open. Al and Dente woke up immediately and scrambled to the door. Chef Claire entered the living room soon after with both Goldens on her heels wagging their tails.

"Hey," Chef Claire said. "I put your dinner in the fridge, Suzy. And I brought some soup for you, Josie. I heard you weren't feeling well. Are you okay?"

"Yeah, I'll be fine," she said. "Thanks for doing that."

"What are you guys up to?"

"We were just getting ready to watch a movie," I said.

"Great. Let me grab a quick shower, and I'll join you."

"Don't be afraid to show them what you've got, girl," Josie said, glancing over at me.

"What?"

"Shut it," I said to Josie, then tossed the remote to Chef Claire. "Find us something good. I think I'm in the mood for a classic."

"Okay," Chef Claire said as she started scrolling through the movie menu. "Here's a good one. From Here to Eternity. We can watch Burt Lancaster and Deborah Kerr make out on the beach."

"No," I said. "Good movie. But I don't like the title."

"Me either," Josie said.

"Okay," Chef Claire said, glancing back and forth at her two weird roommates. "How about Blade Runner?"

"Replicants?" I said, frowning. "No, too close for comfort."

"I agree."

"What?" Chef Claire said, thoroughly confused. "Oh, here's one of my favorites. Alien."

"No. Science fiction is out of the question."

"Absolutely. No science fiction."

"Okay, no sci-fi," Chef Claire said, as she continued to scroll through the list. "How about romance? You guys in the mood for melancholy?"

"I might be a bit overloaded with that at the moment," Josie said.

"No, hang on. That could work," I said. "It might be just what we need. If we watch somebody with bigger problems than ours, it might just be the ticket."

"Maybe you're right."

"How about Ghost?" Chef Claire said.

"Forget it," I said, shaking my head.

"Not gonna happen," Josie said.

"Heaven Can Wait?"

"No," Josie and I said in unison.

"Then why don't one of you guys pick the movie?" Chef Claire said.

"No, keep going. We'll find something," Josie said.

"Maybe a comedy," I said.

"Yeah. Good idea," Josie said, nodding. "I could use a good laugh."

"Okay, classic comedy," Chef Claire said, scrolling. "Let's see what we've got. Here we go. Ghostbusters."

Josie and I looked at each other and nodded.

"Who you gonna call?"

"Perfect."

Chapter 8

I was in the middle of saying hello to all the dogs at the Inn when Josie stuck her head through the door that led into the reception area. Her mood, while still subdued, was better this morning, and she'd managed to wolf down all of her breakfast and half of mine. As such, I was confident she was going to survive yesterday's ordeal.

"What's up?" I said, stepping out of the basset hound's condo and giving her one last head scratch before I closed the door.

"Our friend is back," she said, nodding for me to follow her.

I quickly washed my hands and headed to the reception area where I spotted Josie staring out the window. I glanced outside and saw the Ibizan sitting on the dock staring back at us.

"What does he have in his mouth?" I said.

"I can't tell," Josie said. "Hey, Sammy. Could you please grab my binoculars? I think they're in the cabinet behind the desk."

Sammy brought them over and handed them to Josie. He glanced out the window and nodded.

"Yup. That's definitely the breed. They're my uncle's favorite dog."

"Okay, I guess that answers one of my questions," Josie said, handing me the binoculars.

I peered through the lens and focused on the object in the dog's mouth. I handed them to Sammy and looked at Josie.

"That's the one," I said.

"Hey, it's a CornBelters hat," Sammy said, frowning as he glanced back and forth at us. "You don't think my uncle is in town, do you?"

"I think it's definitely a possibility," I said. "But why the heck does the dog have the hat in his mouth?"

"Good question," Josie said. "And I have another one. Why does he keep coming back here?"

"I don't know," I said. "Maybe we should try thinking like a dog."

"Knock yourself out," Josie said, laughing. "But try to stay away from the toilet."

"Shut it," I said. "And for the record, that's disgusting."

"That's what I keep trying to tell Captain."

"Maybe he's seen all the dogs out in the play area," Sammy said as he watched the dog sitting calmly on the dock.

"That could be it," I said.

"Just think about all the dogs we've got. The smells must be overpowering," Sammy said.

"Uh-oh," I said, frowning.

"Uh-oh, what?" Sammy said.

Josie frowned and looked over at me.

"Uh-oh, what?" Sammy repeated.

"The smell. And the dog has the hat. Let me see those again."
I said, holding them up to my eyes. "The hat is filthy." I lowered
the binoculars and looked at her.

"Dirt?" Josie said.

"Yeah."

"You're saying the dog might have dug the hat up?" Sammy
said. "That it was buried?"

"It's a possibility," I said. "But don't read too much into that,
Sammy. The dog might have just found it on the ground."

"My uncle never took his hat off. And what are the odds there
are two people walking around wearing a CornBelters cap?"

"They're pretty low," I said, shrugging. "It's not like we're
talking about the Yankees here."

"So, what are we going to do?" Josie said. "There's no way
we're going to be able to catch him."

"Maybe he wants us to follow him," I said.

Josie frowned but remained silent as I continued to try and
talk my way into a plan.

"Yesterday morning, after he jumped over me on the dock,
he raced across the lawn and then he made a right."

"Did you see where he ended up?" Sammy said.

"No, it's was too dark. But he definitely turned right."

"Well, the only thing on that side once you get past the play
area are the woods," Josie said.

"We might as well check it out," I said, shrugging. "I can't
think of anything else to do at the moment."

"You don't have a plan?" Josie said.

"Does it sound like I have a plan?" I snapped.

"There's no need to get snarky, Snoopmeister," Josie said. "Geez, I was just asking the question."

"Sorry," I said. "I think we should split up."

"Good idea," Josie deadpanned. "We can do more damage that way."

"Ghostbusters, right?" Sammy said, laughing.

"Yeah, we watched it last night," Josie said.

"Jill and I watched it the other night. It holds up pretty good," Sammy said, nodding.

"Yeah, it does," Josie said. "I was hoping to pick up a few pointers, but I got nothing."

"What?" Sammy said.

"Nothing."

"Will you forget about the movie?" I said, still agitated. "How about you two position yourself on the far end of the play area while I head down to the dock? I'll take a leash with me. Maybe he'll be calmer today and let me bring him up to the Inn. But if he heads for the woods, try to follow him with the binoculars. If we get a good idea which direction he goes in, maybe we can follow his trail."

"Well, it's not the Battle of Trafalgar," Sammy said, shrugging. "But I guess it's better than nothing."

We both stared at him.

"The Battle of Trafalgar?" Sammy said. "One of the greatest battle plans ever executed. I've been reading a lot of military history lately. Never mind. I'll go grab some stuff we might need, and I'll meet you in the play area."

We watched him head off, both of us thoroughly confused.

"He's reading military history now?" Josie said. "This is the same kid who, on his first day, thought the jar of dog biscuits on the reception counter were cookies?"

"Yeah, he's on a real self-improvement kick, isn't he?" I said. "Good for him. And we'll need to go easy on him. If we find a body buried in the woods, and it turns out to be his uncle, things are going to get really strange around here."

"Oh, you mean there might be more to come? I can't wait," Josie said, reaching into the pocket of her scrubs to retrieve her phone. She glanced down at the number. "It's Summerman. The fourth time he's called this morning."

"Aren't you going to answer it?" I said.

"Not a chance," she said.

"You're punishing him?"

"No, I'm not punishing him. This situation isn't his fault. I'm just avoiding him until I'm ready to talk."

"Tomato, tomahto."

"Yeah, like I'm going to take relationship advice from someone who's about to start showering fully clothed."

I made a face at her and headed for the front door.

"Let's go catch a dog," I said.

Chapter 9

I headed for the dock, paused halfway down the lawn to turn around and check if Josie and Sammy were in position, then gave them a quick wave and focused on the dog that was sitting on his haunches and staring back at me. I stepped onto the dock and paused again. The dog appeared calm but didn't take his eyes off me. The baseball hat was laying on the dock right in front of the dog, and he was guarding it like he would his favorite toy. I took a step forward as I reached into my pocket for one of the treats I'd brought along. Judging from the way he leaned forward and stared at it, I thought I'd hit the motherlode. This approach, used to encourage and reward the behavior you wanted to see, was an oldie but a goodie, and we used it around the Inn on a daily basis.

When in doubt, offer them food.

And it always worked like a charm whenever I used it on Josie.

The dog took a step toward me, sniffed the air, and stared at the treat I was holding. I inched closer, and the dog snatched the hat off the dock and slowly began walking toward me. He kept coming using a slow, steady walk that developed into a trot. Then I realized that the dog wasn't heading my way to say hello or have a snack. Rather, he was using the long dock like an airplane uses a runway to build up the necessary speed for takeoff. The dog accelerated, and I froze in my tracks and, once again, watched the dog sail effortlessly over me.

I turned around to watch him race across the lawn, then he turned right, headed around the outside of the play area fence and disappeared from sight. I started to jog across the lawn, tried to ignore my shortness of breath, then stopped when I got a stitch under my ribcage and couldn't go any further. I bent at the knees gasping for air then continued across the grass at a speed that, if you were generous, might possibly be classified as a leisurely stroll. Eventually, I made it to the play area. I draped an arm across the top rail of the fence, breathing heavily.

"Let me guess," Josie said, laughing. "You're about to tell me that you really need to get to the gym."

"Shut it," I said, sucking air into my lungs. "How on earth did I get this far out of shape?"

"Cookies and couches," she said, then cocked her head. "Hey, that would be a great title for a country song. What rhymes with couch, Sammy?"

"Ouch."

"That works. She's definitely in pain."

"Slouch."

"Without a doubt," Josie said, laughing.

"Very…funny," I said, my chest heaving.

"Grouch."

"It won't be long now."

"Shut it," I snapped, glancing around. "Did you see the dog?"

"Only for a second," Sammy said. "That guy can run. We've got a pretty good idea of the direction, but once he got into those woods who knows where he went."

"I really don't feel like spending the rest of the day wandering around in the trees," Josie said.

"Me either," I said, then spotted the baseball cap on the ground near the fence. "Hey, he dropped the hat." I bent over to pick it up, felt my stitch return and groaned. I grabbed the hat, grimaced as I stood upright, and rubbed my side.

"Pitiful," Josie deadpanned as she watched me continue to struggle with my breathing. "Can I get you something? Water? A towel to wipe off the sweat? Oxygen tank?"

"You're...really...not...funny."

"Dis...a...gree."

Sammy laughed as he stared out at the edge of the thick woods that ran for several acres off the back of our property.

"What do you want to do?" he said. "We'd need Smokey the Bear to help us track him down in there."

"Yeah," Josie said. "Or a tour guide."

A light bulb went on, and I glanced at the Inn.

"Duh," I said, shaking my head in disbelief that we'd missed it.

"I smell burning neurons," Josie said. "What is it?"

"We've got our own tour guide," I said.

"What?"

"Bailey," I said. "And we've got the hat."

"Of course," Josie said, nodding. "We've got a bloodhound. The dog has been carrying the hat around in his mouth for at least a day. And since the guy was always wearing it, Bailey shouldn't have any problems following the scent."

"Piece of cake," I said.

"You're such a tease."

"Sammy, would you mind heading down to the Inn and getting Bailey?"

"No problem. Should I put him on a lead?"

"No, but you better bring one along," I said. "And bring a towel and a couple bottles of water, please."

"Oxygen tank?" he said, grinning at Josie.

"Shut it."

We watched him jog toward the Inn, and I wiped my brow with my sleeve. Then I heard Josie's phone buzz again. She checked the number, shook her head, then slid the phone back into her pocket.

"Persistent," I said. "You gotta give him that."

"I don't want to talk about it."

"Fair enough," I said. "Here comes your friend."

Bailey, the bloodhound we'd rescued during our trip to the Caymans, had spotted Josie and was racing across the play area toward her. Josie opened the gate and stood waiting with a huge smile on her face. To say the bloodhound had bonded with her was like saying there was a lot of water in the St. Lawrence. And while Bailey loved being around people and was very friendly to everyone, he absolutely adored Josie. He arrived in a hurry and put his front paws on her shoulders briefly knocking her off balance.

I handed the baseball hat to Josie, and she held it in front of the bloodhound's nose. He immediately began sniffing the air like Josie and I did every time Chef Claire was making dinner. Josie continued to hold the hat close to his nose, and soon Bailey had picked up the scent on the ground and was pulling against the grip Josie had on his collar.

"Okay, I think he's got it," Josie said. "Sammy, hand me the lead, please."

Josie attached the leash to the bloodhound's collar, and Bailey quickly pulled it tight and almost ripped it out of her hand.

"Bailey! Settle," Josie commanded.

The dog sat down in the grass and looked up sheepishly at Josie.

"Good boy," she cooed as she gave him a treat. "He's still getting adjusted to having to listen to somebody. But he's doing good. Aren't you, Bailey?"

The dog thumped his tail on the ground, then stood and made it clear he was ready to get the search started. Josie started walking with Bailey leading the way. Sammy and I followed behind.

"Are you okay?" I said to him when I noticed the look of concern on his face.

"Yeah, I think so," he said, scuffing the grass with his foot. "But if it is my uncle, I've got a whole bunch of questions. He left

Normal two or three years ago, and I don't think anybody has heard a word from him. I know I haven't. And why would he show up here?"

"Maybe he was hoping to reconnect with you," I said. "And maybe it's not even him."

"You mean, a fan of the Normal CornBelters just happened to be passing through town with the same dog? You already said it was highly improbable that it isn't him."

"I don't know what to tell you, Sammy," I said. "But based on recent experience, I wouldn't rule out highly improbable just yet."

We reached the edge of the thick woods and were soon surrounded and dwarfed by the tall pines. The pine smell was overpowering at first, and I wondered if it might throw Bailey off the trail. But the dog continued weaving his way through the maze of trees with his head down and nose close to the ground. Then he veered left, and we did our best to keep up with him.

"How are you holding up?" I said to Josie who continued to be pulled forward.

"I think I snapped a shoulder tendon on that last turn," she said, laughing as she glanced back at us. "This guy is strong."

Then the dog lurched to a sudden stop and Josie stumbled forward. She almost tripped over the dog who was staring down at the bed of pine straw and a pile of dirt directly in front of him. Josie knelt down and petted the dog's head. The bloodhound was panting heavily and seemed agitated.

"Good boy, Bailey. Easy does it."

Josie glanced back at us and nodded. Sammy and I slowly approached and peered over her shoulder. A shallow hole, half uncovered was a few feet away, and it was impossible to miss the lifeless hand that was sticking out of the dirt.

"Is that a watch?" Sammy said.

"Yes, it is," Josie said.

"It's not a Mickey Mouse watch by any chance, is it?" he whispered. Then he said by way of explanation. "He loved that watch. He said it made him feel like a kid again."

"Yeah, I'm afraid it is. I'm so sorry, Sammy," Josie said, climbing to her feet to hug him.

I did the same, but it didn't stop the torrent of tears that began to stream down Sammy's face. He knelt down and examined the watch without touching it.

"Ah, Uncle Johnny. What the heck did you do?"

"Sammy, why don't you take the rest of the day off? You and Jill should do something fun. Maybe take the boat out."

"No," he said, shaking his head. "I need to be here."

"Okay, that's your call," I said, reaching for my phone. I dialed and waited. "Hi, Chief. It's me. Look, I need you to head over to the Inn. We're in the woods off the back of the play area...Yeah. And you better bring Freddie with you...Thanks."

I put my phone back in my pocket and glanced around the peaceful setting that was quiet except for the sounds of chirping birds. They were starting to make quite a racket, and I wondered if they were cranky about us intruding into their space or whether the news of the dead guy was starting to work its way through the forest. I draped an arm around Sammy's shoulder who continued to stare down at the ground. Bailey sat down at Josie's feet, then barked once when he caught a glimpse of the Ibizan standing about twenty feet away.

The Beezer took a tentative step toward us, then another. Soon, it was standing a few feet away, and Sammy extended his hand. The dog sniffed it, then inched even closer. The dog pawed at the dirt and let loose with a high-pitched wail of loss and despair that broke my heart. Sammy knelt down and stroked the Ibizan's head. The dog licked his hand, then eagerly devoured the treats Sammy was offering in rapid succession.

"I don't think he's eaten in a while," Sammy said.

"When you're ready, why don't you get him on a lead and take him down to the Inn?" Josie said. "Give him a bath, get some food and water into him, and then get him settled into one of the condos. I'll check him out as soon as we finish up with the police."

"Maybe I should do that now," Sammy said, slipping the lead over the Beezer's head. "I'll be back as soon as I can."

"Don't worry about it," I said.

"No, I need to be here."

We watched him slowly lead the dog out of the woods.

"Poor kid," I said.

"Yeah. I guess there's nothing like finding a family member buried in a shallow grave," she said, exhaling loudly.

"This is going to be a hard one," I said.

"They're all hard," she said, petting the bloodhound. "You just usually make it look easy."

"Thanks," I said, shaking my head at the crime scene. "The Beezer led us here, right?"

"I think he did," Josie said. "Did you see how he calmed down as soon as we found the body? It was almost like he realized his work was done."

"Yeah," I said, staring down at the shallow grave. "But ours is just getting started."

Chapter 10

Chief Abrams and Freddie, Clay Bay's medical examiner, arrived together about fifteen minutes later. We said quiet hellos, and then they went to work examining what they could see of the body without disturbing the crime scene. Josie and I sat on the ground with our backs against pine trees, and Bailey stretched out between us. He kept a close eye on both two men who chatted quietly for several minutes as they went about their business.

"Okay," Chief Abrams said as he approached. "We're going to need to get a crew out here to dig the body up. You guys don't need to be here for that."

I glanced at Josie who nodded, and we climbed to our feet.

"And Sammy is convinced it's his uncle?"

"Yeah, between the hat and the watch, he's pretty sure," I said, handing over the baseball cap to the Chief. "And he said he wants to be here."

"Yeah, I get that," Chief Abrams said. "But see if you can keep him down at the Inn. Tell him I'll stop by and update everyone before I leave. Sammy doesn't need to watch his uncle's body being dug up."

"Thanks, Chief," I said.

"Okay, that's all I can do for now," Freddie said, walking over and coming to a stop next to the Chief.

"What's your take?" I said.

"It's hard to pin it down until I can get a closer look," he said. "But judging from the rigor in his hand and arm, I'm going to guess he died a couple of days ago. Three at the most."

"Was it one of your dogs that dug him up?" Chief Abrams said.

"No, it was the Ibizan. We're pretty sure it was the victim's dog," I said.

"The dog led you here?" Chief Abrams said.

"We think so," I said, nodding.

"Smart dog," he said.

"He's a grieving dog at the moment. You should have heard the howl he let out earlier," Josie said.

"I wonder if Wally would howl like that if anything ever happened to me?" Chief Abrams said.

Wally was the Chief's basset hound who we'd been taking care of since he was a puppy. And he was a notorious howler, a trait the Chief's neighbors never let him forget.

"Of course, he would. Wally howls when you leave him to go to the kitchen for a fresh beer," Josie said, laughing.

"Yeah, he is kind of a baby, isn't he?" the Chief said, grinning as he reached for his phone. "Hey, Carl. Yeah, it's me. Look, I'm going to need you to grab a couple of guys and headed over to the Doggy Inn...It's a *digging* job... No, there's no need for a backhoe. You'll just need shovels...Yeah. We're in the woods behind the dogs' play area...Just call me when you hit the edge of the woods, and I'll give you directions from there…Thanks. Oh, and Carl, keep this one to yourself, okay? Great. I'll see you then."

The Chief put his phone away and glanced around.

"I've never been back here. It's nice and peaceful. Is this part of your property?"

"No, it belongs to somebody else," I said.

"Who owns it?" Chief Abrams said, glancing back and forth at us.

I looked at Josie, and she shrugged.

"You know, I have no idea," I said, surprised. "How about that? All these years and we never bothered to find out."

"It's always just been The Woods," Josie said. "Apart from the high school kids who come out here to hook up, there's never anybody here."

"We should probably find out," I said, nodding as I looked at Chief Abrams. "That might be a good place to start, huh?"

"Nothing gets past you," he said, grinning.

Josie snorted.

"Shut it."

"Why are you yelling at me?"

"I was talking to him."

Chapter 11

I stared straight ahead and silently cursed my own stupidity. A can-do attitude is all well and good, but when it's combined with a complete lack of foresight, the combination can be deadly and leave you cramped and sweaty in a tin can that had no business being airborne, much less traveling close to three hundred miles an hour, four miles above the ground I couldn't wait to kiss.

After Chief Abrams and I had come up empty in our search for clues about who might have killed Sammy's uncle, we'd been chatting about our possible next steps, and he wondered aloud if it might be a good idea for someone to check out the victim's hometown. And with my Snoopmeter redlining, in my haste to do whatever I could to solve the crime, I'd not only praised Chief Abrams for having such a great idea but had volunteered to handle it.

Unfortunately, I'd forgotten one very important and basic fact. Normal, Illinois was over 700 miles from Clay Bay and would take around fourteen hours of non-stop driving to get there. Including the return trip and the time required to do whatever snooping was required, I would need at least three days away from the Inn, free time I didn't have given the fact that we were entering our busy season.

And when I decided that driving was out of the question, my lack of foresight raised its ugly head when I realized that we'd have to fly. After researching every available flight to Normal departing out of a half-dozen airports, our required travel time, including layovers and connecting flights, had been cut to six hours in each direction, not counting the time required to drive back and forth to the airports. As such, the option of flying was only marginally better. And when the fact that I'd actually have to get on an airplane was added to the mix, fourteen hours in a car was starting to sound like the least objectionable option.

Desperate, I was about to propose using Skype sessions to speak with an as yet unidentified group of people when Josie casually suggested that I charter a plane. We'd be able to fly non-stop on a direct route and be in Normal in less than three hours. Then she reminded me of the private jet we'd taken home from the Caymans, and I was immediately intrigued by the idea. If I was destined to die in a fiery plane crash, I figured I might as well do it while sitting in luxurious comfort.

When she offered to handle all the arrangements, I should have known she was up to something. But I agreed to let her make the reservation, and when we showed up at a small private airstrip this morning, instead of the sleek Gulfstream I'd envisioned, I saw a six-seater Cessna waiting for us. Before I could recover from my shock and berate her for pulling such a cruel stunt, she grinned and gave me a finger wave and drove off before I could get my hands on her.

And that was how I came to be sitting upright in my seat with a frozen stare on my face as the engine droned and the tiny craft worked its way westward through a stiff headwind that rattled the wings and pulled my stomach into my throat. I snuck a quick peek out the window, decided that was a bad idea, and resumed my intricate study of the floral pattern on the seat back directly in front of me.

"I take it you don't like to fly very much."

"What was your first clue?"

"My right hand has gone numb."

"Sorry."

I let go, unceremoniously brushed his hand off the armrest, then regripped. I squeezed both hands as hard as I could to test the strength of my death grip, then nodded. I knew it wouldn't be enough to save me if we crashed, but at least they'd have my fingerprints to help identify the body.

"And for the record, it's not the flying that bothers me. It's the thought of crashing into a mountain."

"No chance of that," Sammy said, laughing. "It's pretty flat throughout the Midwest."

"Then I'm gonna go with crashing into a cornfield," I snapped. "Don't nitpick, Sammy."

I didn't kiss the tarmac when we landed a half-hour later, but I did give it a flirtatious wave as I headed for the terminal. We rented a car, and I tossed the keys to Sammy. Since he was familiar with the area, I stretched out in the passenger seat and looked out the window trying to get a feel for the place. He was right about not having to worry about crashing into a mountain, the place was flat, and corn was sprouting in early summer abundance. We passed a sign for Normal that told us around 50,000 people lived here, and, based on what I saw on the drive from the airport, I was pretty sure the town was aptly named.

"How did the town get its name?" I said, glancing over at Sammy.

"There are all sorts of bad jokes about that," he said, lowering the volume on the radio. "And they get old in a hurry if you live here, so I'll spare you."

"Thanks."

"Normal used to be North Bloomington, but then they decided to split off. And there was a school back then called Illinois State Normal University. Apparently, the normal part is some sort of French reference."

"Sure," I said. "Ecoles Normales. They're secondary education schools for teachers."

"That's right, I forgot," Sammy said, nodding. "You're fluent in French."

"Oui, mais je n'ai pas la possibilité de l'utiliser autant que je le souhaite."

"Yeah, whatever," Sammy said, shrugging.

I laughed and stretched my back.

"So when the town split off, they took the name from the school. Then the school got renamed Illinois State University and the normal reference sort of got lost."

"That's where you went to school?"

"Yeah, that was it. One year. Go, Redbirds."

"It's not the Red Booby, is it?"

"What?"

"Nothing. Just a bad memory," I said, yawning. "What time does the game start?"

"One-thirty," he said, glancing at his watch. "I thought we'd just eat at the ballpark."

"Oh, no. Hot dogs and cold beer?" I said, glancing over. "Not the briar patch. Are you sure we won't have trouble getting tickets?"

"No, it's a day game, and the place holds around seven thousand. We'll be fine. And I used to know all the people who worked at the ticket office. Hopefully, at least one of them is still there."

I nodded and leaned back in my seat. Sammy drove from memory, all of them good judging by the smile on his face, and soon he pulled into the parking area in front of the stadium. I put on a long-sleeved shirt, checked to make sure I had sunscreen in my bag and put my sunglasses on.

"No hat?" Sammy said, frowning.

"I'm going to buy one of the CornBelters hats," I said, following him toward the ticket office.

"Sammy!" a man behind the glass said. "What the heck are you doing here?"

"I thought I'd check to see how my cousin is doing," Sammy said, reaching through the opening to shake the man's hand.

"He's doing good. He plays a mean third base, but he ain't hittin' a lick. Maybe he'll start coming around now that the weather is improving."

"How have you been, Carlos?"

"Great, just great. And you?"

"I'm doing good. Oh, I'd like you to meet my boss, Suzy Chandler."

"Your boss? I was hoping you were gonna tell me she was your girlfriend," he said, grinning. "Nice to meet you."

"You too," I said. "And if you could see his girlfriend, you wouldn't be saying that."

"Still the ladies man, huh, Sammy?" he said, grinning.

"Ladies, man?" I said, glancing over at a red-faced Sammy. "You've been holding out on us."

"Shut it."

"So, I guess you folks need a couple of tickets."

"We do," Sammy said. "You got any good ones left?"

"As a matter of fact, I do. I just had a couple of the Big League Scout seats turned back in. Bobby can't make it today, and he didn't want to see them go to waste."

"Are you kidding?" Sammy said. "That's great."

"Translation, please," I said.

"The Big League Scout seats are right behind home plate. And I mean right behind home. How much are they going for?"

"They're fifty bucks each," Carlos the ticket seller said.

"Fifty bucks?" I said, staring at him in disbelief. "For a minor league baseball game?"

"They include unlimited food and drink," Carlos said, raising an eyebrow.

"Where do I sign?" I said, reaching for a credit card.

Chapter 12

I set the size adjuster on the back of my new hat to its widest setting, slid my ponytail through the opening, and pulled the hat down over my forehead. I beamed at Sammy, proud as a peacock.

"How do I look?"

"Actually, quite normal," Sammy said, nodding.

"Good, I want to blend in," I said, glancing around. "Where the heck is she?"

"Relax, they said she'd be right with us," Sammy said, staring out at the field.

"Which one is your cousin?"

"Number twelve," Sammy said, pointing.

I glanced over at the young man who was holding a bat and listening carefully to the instructions he was receiving from a gray-haired man. Then he took a few practice swings, and I frowned. Sammy noticed, and he sat back in his chair and stared at me.

"What's the matter?"

"I think he's overstriding," I said as I continued to watch the coaching session.

"I didn't know you were into baseball," Sammy said.

"I guess you could say I'm kind of a fan. But my dad was a fanatic. Over the years, I couldn't help but pick a few things up."

"Did you play?"

"Me?" I said, laughing. "No, only in my head. My athletic ability is confined strictly to the mental side of the game. Oh, good. Here she comes."

A young woman approached and stopped next to us.

"Welcome to the Corn Crib. I'm Judy, and I'll be taking care of you today. Great seats, huh?"

"They're amazing," I said, nodding. "Let's see, for starters, I'm thinking a hot dog, burger, and a bratwurst with onions, an order of fries, and a couple of your coldest beers. Oh, and you might as well bring me one of the ears of corn. I can't very well come here and not try the corn, right?"

"You got it," the waitress said.

"What are you gonna have, Sammy?"

The waitress did a double take and stared at me.

"That's all for you?"

"Changing time zones always makes me hungry," I said, shrugging.

"What's your secret for staying so thin?" she said, laughing.

"I worry a lot," I said, grinning. "And what a nice thing to say."

"Well, I am working for tips," the waitress said, then turned to Sammy. "What can I get you?"

Sammy ordered half of what I did, and a few minutes later the waitress returned with our order. Seconds later, we were stuffing our faces.

"You didn't tell your cousin you were coming, did you?" I said through a mouthful of fries.

"No, I thought I'd surprise him," Sammy said. "And I have no idea how I'm going to break the news that his dad is dead."

"I thought we'd take him out for an early dinner after the game. We'll find a nice quiet place where the two of you can talk," I said, then I sat forward in my seat. "Strike? Are you kidding me, ump? That was half a foot off the plate."

Several people sitting nearby laughed at my sudden outburst. A few others moved a couple of rows back to put a bit of space between us. I continued to harangue the umpire behind the plate, and when I made the comment that he might need a seeing eye dog to help him out, he flinched, and briefly glanced over his shoulder.

"Man, you really get into this, don't you?" Sammy said.

"Yeah, it's why I had to stop going to games. There's just something about being in this environment that gets my competitive juices going. This is my first game since the incident in Toronto three years ago."

"Incident?" Sammy said, raising an eyebrow.

"Yeah, Josie and I went to a Blue Jays game, and we sort of got into it with a Red Sox fan."

Sammy sat quietly and waited for me to continue.

"The guy was mouthing off the whole game, and I eventually got tired of listening to him. Then he threw his beer in my face."

"Why did he do that?"

85

"Retaliation, primarily."

"What did you do?" Sammy said, laughing.

"Between innings, I just happened to be walking behind his seat and *accidentally* dropped my ice cream cone down the inside of his shirt."

"Were you drunk?"

"No, just full. And it wasn't one of my favorite flavors," I said, shrugging. "So, no great loss."

"What happened after he threw his beer at you?"

"Josie decked him," I said, laughing at the memory. "He went over the row in front of him and landed, face-down, in a plate of nachos. They caught it on the Jumbo-Tron, and Josie got a standing ovation. But then security asked us to leave and not come back." I glanced back at the action. "What? You have got to be kidding me. On what planet is that a strike?"

At the end of the half-inning, I'd just started working on my second beer when I noticed the umpire strolling toward me. I glanced at him over the top of my cup and smiled at him.

"What are you doing, lady?" the umpire said, softly.

"What do you mean?"

"Why are you busting my chops?"

"I'm merely commenting on the action," I said, turning defensive. "Doesn't dealing with people like me come with the job?"

"Lady, it's in the nineties, I've got a wicked case of acid reflux, and the pollen count is off the charts. You ever try sneezing while you're wearing a catcher's mask over your face?"

"No."

"Well, take it from me, I don't recommend it," he said, blowing his nose.

"Did you take a Zyrtec today?" I said.

"No, I left them in the hotel," he said, wiping his eyes.

I fumbled through my purse and slid two tablets through the protective netting. He stared at me, then popped both tablets and washed them down with a bottle of water.

"Thanks," he said.

"You're welcome."

"Now do me a favor and dial it down a notch," he said, strolling back toward home plate.

"He seems nice. Allergies *and* acid reflux. Poor guy," I said, focusing on my ear of corn. "This is delicious. Oh, look. Your cousin is leading off the inning."

"What's it like living with your brain?" Sammy said, shaking his head at me.

"Probably a lot like sneezing while wearing a mask," I said. "C'mon Tony! Get a hit."

Sammy's cousin looked around confused and saw me waving my arm at him. Then his frown turned into a big grin when he recognized the young man sitting next to me. He walked over to us.

"Sammy. What the heck are you doing here?"

"I just came to watch you go hitless, what else?" Sammy said, laughing.

"Well, I'm sure you won't be disappointed," Tony said, only half in jest. "How are you doing?"

"I'm good. Really good," Sammy said. "Hey, we want to take you to dinner after the game. By the way, this is Suzy. She's my boss."

"Dinner sounds great. Nice to meet you, Suzy."

"You too, Tony. I was watching you earlier, and it looks like you might be overstriding a bit."

"Does it now?" he said, grinning at Sammy.

"Yeah. I think you are. And we both know what that means," I said, nodding.

"We do, huh?"

"Yes. Your weight's getting too far forward and that means your hands are late."

He flinched, and the smile on his face disappeared.

"Thanks for the tip," he said, gripping his bat tight. "I'll just add that one to the hundred other swing thoughts I'm trying to remember."

"I'm not trying to upset you," I said. "It's only a suggestion. Just forget about everything else except making a shorter stride."

"You work for her?" Tony said to Sammy.

"Yeah."

"Doing what? Handing out free advice pamphlets to complete strangers?"

"Funny," I said. "But I would have thought a guy batting ninth and struggling to hit two hundred would be looking for help anywhere he could get it."

"Look, I hate to be rude, but I need to get to the plate," Tony said. "I guess I'll see you guys later. Just meet me outside the clubhouse."

"Will do," Sammy said.

"Suzy, it was a *pleasure* meeting you," Tony said, shaking his head at me.

"Yeah, me too," I said. "Remember, short stride."

"Tenacious, isn't she?" Tony said to Sammy.

"You have no idea."

"Oh, Tony," I said.

He stopped and turned around to look at me.

"The pitcher has started off six of the first eight hitters with a changeup. If I were you, that's what I'd be looking for."

"Got it," he said, bewildered. "Short stride. Look for a changeup. Anything else?"

"Maybe you should try to unclutter your head," I said, shrugging.

"Well, that should be easy enough. Now that you're in there, I doubt if there's room for anything else," he said, heading for the plate.

I took a sip of beer and settled back in my seat. Tony hit the first pitch off the fence in left-center and trotted into second with a stand-up double. He grinned, pointed at us, and gave me a small bow.

"Unbelievable," Sammy said, laughing as he clapped along with the crowd.

"He just needed to get out of his head," I said.

"Well, if anybody would know about that…"

"Funny," I said, then hollered. "Strike? You must be joking. What's the matter, ump? Is all the pollen getting in your eyes?"

Chapter 13

Tony suggested an Italian restaurant known for its food and quiet ambiance, and I sat at the bar talking and flirting with the bartender while he and Sammy chatted in the dining room.

"Let me get this straight," the bartender said. "You run a hotel for dogs and a restaurant?"

"Well, the hotel is only part of the dog business. My partner is a vet, so we offer all those services. And we also have a big rescue program."

"That's kind of a weird combination wouldn't you say?" the bartender said, topping off my glass of club soda.

"Not if you love dogs and food," I said, shrugging.

"Yeah, I guess. And you're about to open more in the Cayman Islands?"

"Yes, we'll be spending the winters down there," I said. "We're all very excited about it."

"And here you are in Normal," he said, laughing.

"Just passing through. But I like it here," I said.

"Yeah, it's nice. But I grew up here, and I'm ready for a change. I'd kill for a chance to work in the Caymans."

"Oh, let's hope not."

"What?"

"Nothing," I said, catching a glimpse of Sammy out of the corner of my eye. "Here comes my dinner date."

"Am I interrupting anything interesting?" Sammy said, grinning.

"None of your business. Are you guys done?" I said.

"Pretty much. I thought I'd give him a few minutes alone before we went back in."

"Of course," I said, nodding. "How did he take the news?"

"It was strange," Sammy said. "I think it hit him pretty hard, but he was…distant. It was like he had already lost his father several years ago. And hearing he was dead seemed to be more about closure than grief."

"People deal with tragedy in a lot of different ways," I said.

"Yeah, I guess. But when my old man died, I was an emotional wreck for a long time. Tony just seems…resigned."

"That's sad."

"Go easy on him with the questions, okay?"

I was hurt that he even had to ask, but I nodded and patted his hand.

"I'll do my best," I said, climbing down off the barstool. "Let's go get some dinner."

"After what you ate at the ballpark. You're still hungry?" Sammy said.

"That's a trick question, right?" I said, leading the way into the dining room.

I sat down across from Tony who was sitting with his elbows on the table and staring off into the distance. But when he saw me, he smiled and sat back in his chair.

"Thanks for the tip today," he said, taking a sip of iced tea. "I can't remember the last time I had three hits in a game."

"It was just a lucky guess on my part," I said, smiling. "How are you doing?"

"I think I'm okay," he said, nodding. "He's pretty much been dead to me for years, but it's still a shock to the system. Sammy said he was murdered."

"Yes, he was."

"I wonder why," Tony said, staring down at the menu in front of him. "He didn't have anything, and he couldn't have been a threat to anybody. Like my mom used to say, he was useless but harmless."

"How long has it been since you saw him?" I said.

"Three years. And the time before that was just after Sammy left. That was five years ago, right, Sammy?"

"Yeah."

"Twice in five years," Tony said. "My mother threw him out, and he just disappeared."

"Does you mom still live around here?" I said, treading carefully with my questions.

"No, she died a couple of years ago. Heart attack," he said, snapping his fingers. "Just like that. She was gone."

"I'm so sorry," I said, as always struggling with what to say during times like this. "Did your father know that she had died?"

"This is going to sound really strange, but I don't have a clue if he knew or not."

"Well, at least he was keeping track of what you were doing," I said.

"Why do you say that?"

"He was wearing a CornBelters hat," I said.

"He was always wearing it," Tony said. "He was a big fan."

"But the one we found was almost new," I said. "Dirty, but pretty new."

"Really?" Tony said.

"I guess he could have ordered it online," I said.

"No way," Sammy said, shaking his head.

"Definitely not," Tony said. "He wouldn't go near a computer. He was convinced that they were designed for mind control. And computers were the way that the aliens were going to take over."

"I've had the same thoughts from time to time," I said, laughing.

"Yeah, but my dad believed it," Tony said.

I glanced back and forth at them. Tony shrugged. Sammy confirmed it with a nod of his head.

"My dad, to be kind, had some bad wiring and more than a few loose screws."

"Do you have any idea about what he was doing in Clay Bay?" I said.

"Not a clue. We did visit one time when I was a kid," Tony said, looking over at Sammy. "That was a fun summer, wasn't it?"

"Yeah, we had a blast," Sammy said. "We were what, seven, maybe eight years old?"

"That sounds about right. After that summer, my dad was always talking about moving there at some point in the future."

"Interesting," I said, leaning forward.

"Not really," Tony said. "He also talked about moving to Mars."

"Sure, sure," I said, reaching for a piece of Italian bread. I broke off a corner and dipped it in olive oil.

"What's your sister up to these days?" Sammy said, also grabbing a piece of bread.

"I have no idea," Tony said. "After mom died, she and I had a major falling out and went our separate ways. Last I heard, she was living somewhere in New York. Some place called Deferiet. I think that's it."

I sat back in my chair and glanced over at Sammy. He seemed as surprised as I was.

"Deferiet? That's not far from Clay Bay," Sammy said.

"Really?" Tony said. "I did not know that. Huh, how about that?"

"What does your sister do?"

"Drugs," Tony said, softly. "She does drugs."

"What kind of drugs?" I said.

"Any kind she can get her hands on," Tony said. "When it comes to dope, my sister doesn't discriminate. But the last time I saw her, she seemed to have a big crush on crystal meth."

"I can't believe she's living in Deferiet," Sammy said. "What's the town like?"

"Well, there used to a big paper mill there. But after it closed, I think the place really went downhill. I haven't driven through there in a long time, but I can't imagine there are more than a few hundred people living there now. Right, Suzy?"

"That sounds about right," I said, trying to organize several thoughts that were racing through my head. "Is there any way your sister would have heard the news about your father?"

"Did it make the local papers?" Tony said.

"I don't think it did yet," I said.

"Then I don't see how she would know."

"Somebody should probably tell her, don't you think?" I said, catching Tony's eyes and holding them with mine.

"Knock yourself out," he said, shrugging. Then he focused on his menu. "I think I'm gonna go with the lasagna."

Chapter 14

Josie was waiting for us at the airstrip just outside of town when we landed. She was leaning against the side of the car and looking way too smug. She waved when the Cessna taxied to a stop, and Sammy and I headed down the small set of stairs and strolled toward her.

"Nice hat," she said, taking both our bags and tossing them in the trunk. "So, do tell. How was your flight?"

"Shut it," I said, climbing into the passenger seat. "I owe you one. A big one."

"Yes, you do," she said, still laughing. "But you're gonna have to dig deep to beat this one."

"How are the dogs?" I said.

"They're all good. Even the Beezer is starting to get comfortable."

"Good. Did you talk with Summerman yet?"

"No. New subject, please," she said, heading for the main road that would take us into town. "Oh, Freddie called this morning. He wants you to stop by as soon as you can."

"Okay," I said, nodding. Then I turned to Sammy in the backseat. "He must have finished with the body. Maybe he found something that might help us figure out who killed your uncle."

"I need to talk to him about getting access to the body," Sammy said. "And then have him cremated and sent to Tony. Since it was one of his uncle's favorite places, Tony said he wants to spread him all over the ballpark."

"Yuk," I said.

"Maybe they could do it as part of a promotion," Josie said.

"Scattered Ashes Night?" I said, frowning.

"Exactly."

"Yuk."

"You can put someone's ashes in the mail, right?"

"I don't see why not," I said, shrugging.

"Or I suppose you could fly back and deliver them personally," Josie deadpanned. "Ow. That hurt," she said, rubbing her shoulder.

"Good. It's supposed to hurt. Sammy, I thought that we might take a drive to Deferiet tomorrow."

"The old paper mill town?" Josie said. "What on earth for?"

"My cousin apparently lives there," Sammy said. "I don't think she knows that her dad died. And her brother doesn't want anything to do with her. But she needs to know."

Josie pulled into the driveway, and we headed directly to the Inn. Sammy got reunited with Jill while I said hello to Chloe and the rest of the dogs. Then I grabbed my bag from Josie's car and headed up to the house. I tossed the bag on my bed, then called Chief Abrams who agreed to meet me at Freddie's office. With Chloe supervising from the passenger seat, we made the short drive, and I parked in front. Chloe led the way inside, and we found Chief Abrams already there talking with Freddie.

"Hey, welcome home," Freddie said.

"Good trip?" Chief Abrams said.

"Not counting the flights, yeah, it wasn't bad," I said, sitting down. "What did you find out, Freddie?"

"At first, nothing," he said, shrugging. "There were no wounds or bruises. Nothing at all. It was almost like the guy died of natural causes."

"But since people who die of natural causes usually aren't buried in shallow graves in the woods, you kept looking, right?" I said, groaning softly when Chloe jumped up on my lap and stretched out.

"That's why you're the Snoopmeister," Freddie said, laughing. "Yeah, I kept looking."

"Something came back on the toxicology report, didn't it?"

"How the heck did you know that?" Freddie said.

"Lucky guess. He didn't happen to OD on crystal meth, did he?" I said, raising an eyebrow.

"You're starting to scare me, Suzy."

"Me too," Chief Abrams said, staring at me. "How on earth did you figure that out?"

"Freddie has another cousin, the daughter of the dead guy who, according to her brother, has a major drug problem."

"And that was all the information you needed to make the connection?" Freddie said. "No way."

"But he did overdose on crystal, right?"

"Yeah, he sure did. He had enough of it in his system to choke a horse," Freddie said. "But there has to be more to the story. If that's all you had to go on, I'm going to start thinking you're psychic."

"The daughter lives in the area," I said.

"Really?" Chief Abrams said. "Where?"

"Last known address, Deferiet."

"Interesting," Chief Abrams said, getting up from his chair to start pacing back and forth.

"Why is it interesting?" Freddie said. "The town pretty much died after the paper mill closed."

"Yes, it did," Chief Abrams said. "And that opened up a lot of opportunities for folks looking for somewhere nice and quiet to set up shop."

"You lost me, Chief."

"Cookers," I said, softly.

"Exactly," Chief Abrams said, nodding.

"Are you telling me that the dead guy and his daughter were cooking meth in downtown Deferiet?"

"No, I doubt very much if they're cooking in town. You can smell that stuff a mile away when it's being made," Chief Abrams said. "Somebody definitely would have noticed."

"But there are a ton of old farmhouses around the area that are nice and remote," I said.

"There certainly are. And they're undoubtedly very cheap to rent," Chief Abrams said. "It wouldn't be hard to find out who is renting mailboxes at the local post office."

"Sammy and I are heading there tomorrow to track her down and break the news about her dad."

"You want me to come along?" Chief Abrams said.

"No, if they are cooking meth, having a cop show up at their door would only make them suspicious."

"Okay, but be careful. And call me if you have any problems. Those crank heads can be mean and very unpredictable."

"Will do," I said, staring out the window deep in thought. "How big a dose did the guy take?"

"It was massive. Four to five hundred milligrams," Freddie said. "That's at least triple the standard amount for an overdose. It was almost like he was trying to commit suicide. Apart from the shallow grave, of course."

"I doubt if he was a willing participant. And with that big of a dose, they weren't taking any chances that he'd survive," Chief Abrams said, helping himself to coffee.

"No, they weren't. The geniuses who killed him shouldn't have bothered burying him," I said. "We probably would have written it off as a suicide. Or an accidental overdose."

"Yeah, I'm sure we would have," Chief Abrams said. "But cookers usually aren't the sharpest tools in the shed."

"Well, this group hasn't blown themselves up yet," I said. "For now, we should probably assume they know what they're doing. But why use the woods behind our place?"

"I took a look yesterday, and there's an access road on the other side of the woods where it would be easy to park a car out of sight. It's a bit of a hike to the spot where we found the body, but it's doable," Chief Abrams said.

"But why those woods?" I said, then a light bulb went off.

"Uh-oh," Freddie said, laughing. "She's got that look."

"Talk to me, Suzy," Chief Abrams said, sitting on the edge of Freddie's desk.

"A boat. Somebody is coming in by boat in the middle of the night. There's a lot of shoreline with decent access about a quarter mile up from us. They're using those woods as a meeting place."

"To do what?" Freddie said.

"To swap meth for cash would be my guess," Chief Abrams said. "So, they're selling to somebody on the Canadian side?"

"That's smart," I said. "If they aren't selling their product locally, that must lower their risk of getting caught, right?"

"It would," he said, nodding. "And as long as they keep a low profile, and nobody gets a whiff of what they're up to – pardon the pun – they should be able to stay below the radar."

"And you think Sammy's uncle was right in the middle of all this?" Freddie said.

"I don't know," I said. "But I have a feeling that, one way or another, the daughter definitely knew her father was around."

102

"And you expect her to lie to you tomorrow when you stop by?" Chief Abrams said, grinning.

"Oh, I'm counting on it."

Chapter 15

Josie was extremely unhappy with me when I told her where I was going, but she settled down when I explained the purpose of my visit. I got up very early to take care of some overdue paperwork, and do a bit of work on a paper we were presenting together at an upcoming conference in Ottawa. And only when the sun had risen far above the horizon did I head down to the dock with Chloe at my heels.

I hopped in the boat, started the new motor, and nodded appreciatively at its quiet purr. With Chloe perched in the seat next to me, I headed for Summerman's island at a speed that produced the least amount of wake. The water level was still high, and it was definitely having an impact on the number of boats on the River. Traffic was very light, and I reached the island in a little over thirty minutes, parked in the boathouse, then heard the sound of a piano coming from the library.

Summerman's dog, Murray, greeted us with a loud woof, then recognized both of us and he and Chloe dashed off to play and explore the island. I tapped on the screen door, and the music stopped.

"Yes?"

"It's me," I said, opening the door.

"Hey, Suzy," Summerman said, getting up to greet me and give me a gentle hug.

"I get a hug? So, you're not still mad at me?"

"No, what's the point of staying mad? Life's too short, right?" he said, grinning.

"For some of us, I suppose."

"Are you here to deliver a message from Josie? She still isn't talking to me."

"Me either," I said. "I mean, she's not talking to me about you."

"Yeah, I got it," he said, sitting back down at the piano. "So, what's up?"

"I just have a few questions about the favor the woman on the other side asked you to do."

"Okay," he said, beginning to play. "But I already told you I wasn't paying close attention to what she was saying."

"Could it have been the guy's ex-wife?"

"I guess it could have been, but I don't think she mentioned it," he said, shrugging as he started to play a complicated progression up and down the keyboard, then stopped, started again, then stopped and stared down at the keyboard. "Geez, I remembered it yesterday. What the heck is going on with my brain today?"

"Sure, brain cramp. I get those all the time."

"I'm sure you do," he said, laughing as he completed the run to perfection. "There we go. That's better. You like it?"

"It's good."

"Thanks. What else have you got for me? I need to get ready. We're heading off for a few days."

"Going anywhere interesting?"

"I'm sure it'll be interesting," he said.

"How about fun?"

"How about you stop asking questions regarding where I'm going?"

"Got it," I said, nodding. "I was wondering if the location she told you to look for the guy in was the woods behind our place."

He stopped playing and stared at me.

"As a matter of fact, it was. How did you know that?"

"That's where we found the body buried."

"Oh, I'm sorry to hear that. I didn't know. How did he die?"

"A massive overdose of crystal meth."

Summerman frowned.

"She didn't mention anything about drugs," he said. "The only thing she said was that he was in over his head on something."

We heard the low woof coming from the other side of the screen door.

"No, you're spoiled enough as it is, Murray," Summerman said. "Open it yourself."

I swear I heard the dog grumble as he tapped the door with a paw, caught the door with his head, then held it open for Chloe to squeeze through before following her inside. Chloe waited for me to pet her and then stretched out next to Murray under the piano.

"He's excited. He knows we're going somewhere," Summerman said. "Murray loves to fly."

"Good for Murray," I said, turning back to the door when I heard another noise.

Two men entered, took a long look at me, then sat down next to each other on the couch. One was older, somewhere in his fifties I guessed, attractive, and seemed to have a pleasant disposition. Except for the eyes, which bore deep as he continued to study me. The other man was one of the smallest adults I'd ever seen, and the best description I could come up with for his mood was *grumpy disinterest*.

"Are you about ready to go?" the older man said. "Captain Bob just called, and he said the plane's all set."

"Almost. I just need to pack a bag," Summerman said. "Doc, Merlin, I'd like you to meet Suzy Chandler. Suzy, this is Doc and Merlin. They're two of my closest friends and colleagues."

"Are they…?"

"Part timers?" Summerman said, laughing. "No."

"I can only wish," Doc said.

"This is the nosy one you've been talking about who can't stop sticking her beak where it doesn't belong?" the small man named Merlin said.

"Nosy is a bit harsh, don't you think, Summerman?" I said. "I prefer the term snoop."

"Call it whatever you want," Merlin said, glaring at me. "Just keep your mouth shut about Summerman."

"Oh, you like to get right to the point," I said, returning his stare. "Usually, I like that in a man, but in your case, I'm going to make an exception."

Doc and Summerman roared with laughter. Merlin didn't find it quite as funny.

"You were right," Doc said to Summerman. "She's great." Then he looked over and gave me the once over. "Maybe you'd like to come work with us."

"Would there be dogs involved?" I said, fighting the urge to flirt with him.

"Only Murray," Doc said.

"Then I'll pass," I said, smiling.

"Good call. If you're as nosy as he says, you wouldn't last a week," Merlin said, giving me a blank stare.

"I don't think I like you," I said through a narrowed-eyed glare.

"Get in line."

Summerman and Doc laughed again.

"You're such a charmer, Merlin," Doc said. "Don't mind him, Suzy. He's been on the wagon for over a year, and he's still mad about having to do it."

"Hey, I've got an idea," Summerman said. "Do we have anything in the database about crystal meth operations around here?"

Merlin shrugged but pulled a device out of his pocket that resembled a cell phone and tapped the keyboard several times. He studied the device as Doc leaned over his shoulder. Merlin scrolled through what I assumed were several screens of data, then glanced over at Summerman.

"We've got a few things," Merlin said. "It's pretty sketchy, but there's been a huge spike in crystal use on the Canadian side. Around Kingston. That's what, thirty miles from here?"

"Yeah, that's about right," Summerman said. "Wasn't there a crank head we used to use occasionally as a snitch? I think he was from Kingston. Remember him?"

"Sure," Doc said. "Tommy Nostril."

"Yeah, Tommy," Summerman said. "Is he still around?"

"Let me check," Merlin said, focusing on the device again. "Yeah, he's still there. You think he's started moving product?"

"It wouldn't surprise me," Doc said. "It's probably the only way he could afford his habit. Why do you want to know?"

"Some guy got killed in Clay Bay, and it looks like there's a meth angle tied into it," Summerman said. "And Suzy is *snooping* for clues."

"What is that thing?" I said, staring at the device Merlin was holding.

"For a snoop like you, this is the Holy Grail."

"Can I see it?"

"No."

"Did you get it from the government?"

109

Merlin snorted derisively.

"They got it from me."

"I see. What sort of information is on it?"

"All of it."

"All of what?"

"The information," Merlin said, frowning. "What do you think I'm talking about?"

"There's no need to get snarky."

"And there's no need for you to ask any more questions," Merlin said.

"Are you always like this?"

"Only when I'm in a good mood," Merlin said. "Now, do you want Tommy Nostril's address or not?"

"Yeah."

"Yeah, what?"

"What?"

"Aren't you going to say the magic word?"

"Oh, I've got a magic word for you. But I don't think you're gonna like it."

Chapter 16

I said my goodbyes to Summerman and Doc and gave Merlin a gesture that I guess could have loosely been considered a wave. I got back to the Inn just in time for lunch and had a sandwich with Josie in my office. She had several questions, most of them Summerman related, but she did perk up when I mentioned the fact that I'd been able to come up with an interesting lead on the Canadian side.

She devoured her sandwich and headed straight into an emergency surgery on a young black Lab that had jumped out the back window of his owner's car, raced onto the local golf course, then tried to swallow a golf ball he'd chased down about 280 yards off the tee on the ninth hole. Apparently, someone had hit the drive of his life, and, while mildly concerned about the well-being of the dog, was more interested in debating with his playing partners whether or not he was entitled to a free drop. But someone else from the foursome had stepped up and helped the owner carry the dog back to the car then drive while she sat in the back seat massaging the dog's windpipe. Eventually, the dog managed to swallow the Titleist, but now the ball needed to be surgically removed.

I filed it away as a story suitable for retelling only if the dog made a full recovery, said goodbye to Chloe, and collected

Sammy from reception on my way out the door. Since we weren't in a hurry, and the weather was good, we decided to avoid the monotony of Interstate 81 and wound our way through the backroads until we hit Route 26 South, then headed east on Route 3 until we arrived in Deferiet about forty minutes later. I drove along the main street and shook my head at the devastating economic impact the closing of the paper mill had caused.

"When I was a kid, my mother always talked about what a great town this was," I said, slowing down to wait for a couple of dogs as they leisurely made their way across the street.

"That old paper mill looks like a bomb hit it," Sammy said. "When did it close?"

"I think it was around 2004, but it had been shrinking for a while. The paper industry starting consolidating in the nineties, and a lot of the small towns with mills bore the brunt."

"What are the people who are still living here doing?" Sammy said.

"Trying to hang on, I imagine," I said, coming to a stop in front of the post office. "Okay, you got your story straight?"

"I do," he said, climbing out of the car.

We headed inside and found the place empty except for an older woman who was sorting a small stack of mail and inserting pieces into various mailboxes. When she saw us waiting at the counter, she approached us with a smile.

"How can I help you?" she said, glancing back and forth at us.

112

I hung back and let Sammy take the lead.

"I'm looking for my cousin who lives in the area, but I don't have her address. I thought she might have a post office box here in town."

"Well, I'm not sure I can give you any information even if she does," the woman said, shrugging. "Privacy and all that. You can understand that, right?"

"Of course," Sammy said, nodding. "And I wouldn't want you to break any rules. But I have some very distressing news to give her. Family news."

"I see," the clerk said. "Distressing news, you say?"

"Yes, it's about her father."

"Okay," the clerk said, thinking hard. "Well, if you give me her name, I guess it wouldn't hurt if I took a look."

"Thanks. Her name is Jolene Anderson," Sammy said.

The clerk let the name roll around in her head, then she shrugged.

"I'll check, but that name doesn't ring a bell," the clerk said. "And as you probably noticed, it's a small town. If somebody is living here and I don't know who they are, I'll be very surprised."

The clerk put her glasses on and tapped her keyboard. She studied the screen then shook her head.

"No, there's nobody renting a box here with that name. Maybe you should check at the post office in Carthage," she said, removing her glasses and tossing them on the counter. "It's not far from here."

"I'm sure she's living around here," Sammy said. "But if I know Jolene, she has a boyfriend. The box is probably in his name."

"What does she look like?" the clerk said.

"Well, this is probably going to sound harsh, what with her being a relative and all, but she's really thin, and her hair is usually sort of greasy and stringy. She's not the most hygienic member of the family. And she has a black and red skull and crossbones tattoo on her right forearm."

"Oh. Her."

"So, you do know Jolene?" Sammy said.

"Only well enough to stay away from her," the clerk snapped, then immediately softened. "I'm sorry, I shouldn't be talking about your cousin like that. At least in front of you."

"It's okay. I understand. Jolene tends to have that effect on most people," Sammy said.

"She and her boyfriend rent the old Wilson place. It's about four miles out of town. Get back on Route 3, head east, then take 37 South. If you hit Fort Drum, you've missed the turnoff. You'll go a couple of miles south on 37, then you'll see a dirt road with an old sign with the Wilson name on it. Take that road until it dead-ends. You'll see the house right off to the right."

"Thank you so much," Sammy said. "You're very kind."

"No problem. Have a nice day," the clerk said, waving as she went back to sorting mail.

We headed outside to the car.

"Interesting reaction," I said.

"Yeah, but not surprising," Sammy said. "Jolene is very much an acquired taste. And I haven't seen her in quite a while. Who knows how much further downhill she's gone."

"How old is she?"

"Let's see," Sammy said, frowning as he did the math. "She's gotta be twenty-five. Yeah, that sounds about right."

"But she doesn't look it, right?"

"Your mom could pass for twenty-five easier than Jolene," he said, shaking his head.

I followed the mail clerk's directions, and a few minutes later I parked the car at the end of a long dirt driveway. We got out of the car and looked around.

"Remote," Sammy said.

"Very. And probably a good spot to do some serious cooking."

I followed Sammy up onto the porch that looked like it was about to detach itself from the rest of the house. A yellow lab with cloudy eyes was stretched out near the door and only managed a soft thump of its tail. He was seriously malnourished, and anger surged through me as I bent down to stroke the dog's head. But I momentarily put my concerns for the dog aside and stood behind Sammy when he knocked on the door. A minute later, the door opened partway, and a haggard face appeared. The woman blinked as the sunlight hit her eyes, and it took her several seconds to focus. Then she recognized the person standing on the porch.

"Sammy?"

"Hi, Jolene. How are you doing?"

"What on earth are you doing here?" she said, slipping through the door and closing it behind her.

They shared a brief hug, and Sammy took a step back. Even though it was close to eighty degrees, she shivered when the gentle breeze hit her.

"Jolene, I'd like you to meet Suzy. She's my boss."

"It's nice to meet you," she said, extending her arm to shake hands.

"Nice to meet you too, Jolene," I finally managed.

I did my best not to stare at her. You could have given me a dozen guesses at her age, and I still wouldn't have come within five years of the right number. To say she was skinny was like saying I had a bit of a thing for dogs. She looked like she hadn't showered in at least a week, her eyes were red and glazed, and, as cruel as it was to have the thought, I was glad I was standing upwind. I noticed the tattoo on her forearm, but what captured most of my attention were the unmistakable needle tracks that ran along the inside of her arm.

"So, what brings you out here?" she said.

"I'm afraid I have some bad news for you," Sammy said.

"Okay," she said, blankly.

"It's about your dad," Sammy said.

I watched her reaction closely and thought I saw her flinch. But she maintained eye contact with Sammy and cocked her head.

116

"What about my father?"

"I'm sorry to tell you this, Jolene. But he's gone."

"Gone?" she said, frowning. "As in dead?"

"Yes. He was murdered. And his body was found buried in the woods right outside of Clay Bay."

"They found his body?" she whispered. "I mean, he was buried?"

"Yes."

Then Jolene summoned up everything she had to produce a few tears. She lowered her head, scratched at her needle tracks, then sat down in a lawn chair that was right next to the door.

"I can't believe it," she said, running her hands through her hair.

I'd soon seen all I needed to of her performance and refocused on the lab whose breathing seemed to be irregular. I glanced up when I heard the front door open.

"Hey, Jolene," a man snapped. "Have you seen my apron? I'm trying to get organized before I cook tonight and I can't find it anywhere."

Then he noticed Sammy and I standing on the porch.

"Who the hell are you?" he said, glancing back and forth at us.

"Carl, this is my cousin, Sammy," Jolene said, obviously relieved to have something else to focus on.

"Your cousin?" he said, then focused on me. "And you are?"

"Really worried about this dog," I said, kneeling down. "When was the last time she ate?"

"What?" the man said. "What business is that of yours?"

"I'm kinda tight with Animal Protection," I said, glaring back at him. Then I gave him my best crocodile smile. "So, here's what I'd like to do. I'm going to take her with us when we leave. But don't worry, I'm sure you won't even realize she's gone."

"No way. I don't think that's gonna happen," Carl said. "Some stranger isn't just gonna show up and take our dog."

"Okay, have it your way," I said, grabbing my phone out of my pocket. "I'll just call their office and report what looks like a severe case of animal abuse. I'm sure they won't mind stopping by with a few of our friends from the state police to take a look around."

Carl broke eye contact, sniffed several times, then looked over at Jolene who nodded at him.

"Knock yourself out," he said, shrugging. "The dog is pretty much worthless."

"I'm sure it's a learned behavior," I deadpanned. "Foot of the master and all that."

"What?" Carl said, confused. "Hey, look lady. I don't think I like-"

"So, you're doing some cooking tonight?" Sammy said, doing his best to de-escalate the situation.

"Huh?" Carl said, then nodded. "Oh, yeah. I'm cooking tonight. Jolene and I are...having a barbecue."

"Really?" I said. "What are you having?"

"You know. Just the usual," Carl said.

"Sounds delicious," Sammy said. "I wish we weren't busy tonight. I'd love to stick around and catch up."

Both Jolene and Carl visibly relaxed and exhaled.

"Carl, Sammy just dropped by to tell me some very bad news about my dad. He died," Jolene said.

"I see. That's too bad. I'm sorry to hear that, Jolene," Carl said, scuffing the porch with the toe of his ratty sneaker. Then he looked at Sammy. "How do you know he's dead?"

"How do I know he's dead?" Sammy said, bewildered. "It's really not that hard to figure out."

"Yeah, sure. What with rigid mortis and all that. What I mean is, did you read about it in the paper? Maybe you got a phone call from somebody in the family."

"Oh, I see where you're going," Sammy said. "No, I saw the body."

"Really?" Carl said, frowning. "How the…I mean, that must have been…quite a shock."

"Yes," I said, unable to contain myself. "*Everyone* is obviously very surprised by the news."

"Well, he had lots of problems," Jolene said. "But I'm sure he's in a better place now."

If her father had been here, and I was sure he had, I had to agree with her comment. Any place other than standing on the porch of this crumbling house with two sniffling junkies who were killing their own dog with willful neglect had to be better.

"I just thought you should know in case you hadn't heard, Jolene," Sammy said.

"I appreciate it, Sammy," she said, choosing her words very carefully. "Do you need me to do anything? You know, like identify the body?"

"I think we got that covered," Sammy said.

"Yeah, of course," she said, flashing a small smile. "Duh."

"Okay, we're going to get out of your hair," Sammy said. "It was nice seeing you. Maybe after things settle down, we'll all get together. Maybe we'll have a barbecue, and I'll get to check out Carl's cooking abilities."

"That would be great, wouldn't it, Carl?"

"Yeah, great."

"Are you ready to go, Suzy?" Sammy said.

"All set," I said, sighing. "I guess it was too much to expect that these guys would know anything about the money. I guess it's back to the drawing board, right?"

Sammy stared at me, confused, but then he caught on and nodded.

"Yeah, back to the drawing board. I don't think we're ever going to find out who it belongs to."

"Money?" Jolene said.

"Yeah," I said, gently stroking the dog's ribcage. "The police found an envelope stuffed with cash next to the body."

"What?" Carl said.

"Yeah," Sammy said. "A whole bunch of cash. How much was it again, Suzy?"

"I think it was around a hundred thousand."

"A hundred grand?" Carl said. "What? How the…why would he have been walking around with that much money?"

"Nobody seems to know," I said.

"It's quite a mystery," Sammy said.

"What's going to happen to the money?" Jolene said.

"I don't know," I said, shrugging. "All they found on the envelope were the initials TN. And that's not much to go on."

"Maybe it'll be donated to a charity," Sammy said.

"Like Animal Protection," I said.

"Exactly. Well, we better get going."

"Hang on," Carl said. "Where's this money at?"

"I think Chief Abrams probably has it," I said. "He's the Clay Bay chief of police."

"Maybe we should talk to him," Carl said. "I mean, what with Jolene being the lawful heir and all that."

"I guess it couldn't hurt," I said, shrugging. "But he'll probably have some questions for you."

"What sort of questions?" Jolene said.

"You know. Just the usual," I said, smiling at Carl. "Whenever the cops find that much cash next to a dead body, their minds tend to drift toward the illegal side of the street. Cops are funny that way."

"Yeah, funny," Carl said.

"It was nice meeting both of you," I said. "We'll catch you later."

I bent down and scooped the dog up into my arms. She was light as a feather, and I headed for the car fighting every urge to head back to the house and kick the crap out of both of them. I gently put the dog in the backseat, tossed the keys to Sammy, and climbed in next to the lab. I located a bag of dog treats and spent the most of the drive home hand feeding them to her one at a time. Then the dog let loose with a contented sigh and fell asleep on my lap. I patted her head, and realized, once again, how easy it was to judge the quality of people just from the way they treated animals.

"You did good, Sammy."

"Thanks. But I feel bad. I kept trying to find a way to feel sorry for her, but I've got nothing but contempt. They're both despicable."

"Yes, they are," I said, stroking the lab's head. "I particularly liked the way she didn't even bother to ask how her father died."

"Yeah, I noticed. So much for the grieving daughter," Sammy said. "Where did you come up with the story about the money? That was brilliant."

"I was looking for a way to screw with what's left of their heads, and I figured that if anything could get them to do something really stupid, it would be thought of getting their hands on a stack of cash."

"You think they're going to get in touch with Chief Abrams?"

"Oh, I'm sure they will. If you were in their shoes, wouldn't you?"

"I don't know," he said, glancing at me through the rear-view mirror. "If I was cooking meth, I'd probably want to keep as much distance as I could between me and the cops."

"Yes, that's what a person with a working brain would do," I said.

"Yeah, you're probably right. Those two are definitely a couple tacos short of a fiesta platter," he said, shaking his head. "Where did you come up the initials? You lost me with that one. Who's TN?"

"Tommy Nostril."

"Should I know who that is?"

"No, definitely not. You've done more than enough. It's time to let the pros handle it from here."

"Oh, so you're gonna back off too?" he deadpanned through the mirror.

"Funny."

Chapter 17

I sat back as the waiter topped off our wine glasses and glanced around the dining room. C's, as it always was on Friday nights, was jam-packed and loud. I took a sip of wine and shook my head in amazement as I watched Josie make short work of her stuffed mushrooms. She set her knife and fork on her plate, wiped her mouth, then took a sip of water and sighed contentedly.

"What?" she said, catching a glimpse of my stare out of the corner of her eye. "Did I spill something on myself?"

"Hard to tell," I said. "Everything is such a blur when you're eating."

"Shut it."

Chief Abrams, sitting between us, chuckled as he worked on his salad.

"So, they finally called you?" I said.

"Yeah, it must have taken them a couple of days to work up the courage," he said, laughing. "Cops and cookers usually only talk when there's an arrest involved."

"How are you going to handle the mysterious hundred grand?" Josie said.

"I thought I'd start by asking them a whole bunch of questions about where the money could have come from and go from there," he said. "It shouldn't take long for them to talk themselves into a corner."

"Good plan," I said, nodding. "How do you want to deal with the mysterious Tommy Nostril?"

"I thought I'd take Sunday off and you and I would take a trip over to Kingston to check out that address."

"As a couple of tourists just visiting, right?"

"Exactly."

"Did you give the Sniffle Twins a specific time to come in?" I said to Chief Abrams.

I wish I could take credit for the nickname we'd given Jolene and Carl, but Josie had come up with it soon after I'd given her the update about our visit the other day.

"They said they'd like to come in as soon as they get up tomorrow," Chief Abrams said.

"Let me guess," I said. "Two-thirty?"

"Close. Three," he said, shaking his head. "They said they work nights and like to sleep in."

"All that night cooking must be exhausting," I said, laughing. "I'll be there before three."

"I'd be shocked if you weren't," he said, taking another bite of his salad.

"Maybe they'll blow themselves up and do all of us a favor," Josie said, starting to work on her salad.

"A bit harsh, don't you think?" Chief Abrams said.

"Not really," she said, shaking her head. "After what they did to that poor dog? If Suzy and Sammy hadn't shown up, she would have died on that porch. She didn't have much fight left in her."

"But she's going to be, okay, right?" Chief Abrams said.

"Eventually," Josie said, staring at her fork. "What is that?"

"Beet," I said, glancing over.

"Since when does Chef Claire put beets in the house salad?"

"She's just doing a test run to see how people like it," I said.

"Well, make her stop," Josie said as she speared all of the intruders with her fork and put them on a separate plate. "The dog will be fine. But I've still got her on an IV. And we'll need to keep slowly increasing her calories."

"So, you can't just feed her what you normally would?" Chief Abrams said.

"No, but that's what a lot of people think they should do. When anything, including people, is starving, you have to be careful about how much you feed them until they're ready for it. The body adjusts to not having food, and if you overdo it too quickly, you can do a lot of damage. Even kill them if you're not careful."

"I did not know that," Chief Abrams said. Then he grinned.

"What's so funny?" Josie said.

"I just never thought I'd be learning about starvation from you," he said.

I snorted and almost spilled my wine.

126

"You're pretty funny for a cop," Josie said, then turned to me. "Oh, I forgot to tell you. When I asked all the summer hires for a volunteer to stay with the lab tonight, Jenny raised her hand again. That'll be four nights in a row. She's totally bonded with the dog and will probably want to adopt her. And she says she wants to pick up all the overtime she can get. So, it's another night down at the Inn for her."

"Better her than us, right?" I said.

"Yeah, we've done more than our share of condo overnighters," Josie said, frowning at her salad. "Yuk. See, that's what I'm talking about. The beet is *bleeding* all over the romaine."

I took a sip of wine and stared off into the distance.

"What?" Josie said.

"Our biggest problem is beets in the salad. How spoiled have we gotten?"

"Suzy, please don't start with the *Don't hate me because I'm rich* thing again. I'm trying to enjoy my dinner."

"I'm not starting anything."

"Whatever you say, Snoopmeister. Look, it's very simple, and it doesn't have anything to do with being spoiled. I hate beets. No, let me restate that just so I'm perfectly clear. I *detest* beets. Beets should be left in the ground to rot. Beets are definitive proof that, when it comes to things you can eat, God definitely has a sense of humor. They're the poster child for why kids shouldn't have to eat their vegetables. In short, beets suck. And I don't want them in my salad. If that makes me spoiled, then just send me to bed without my dinner. But since my dinner has beets in it, I guess I should thank you for doing that. That's all I'm saying. No beets. End of story. Pass the bread, please."

"Okay, we got it," I said, shaking my head as I handed her the bread basket. "No beets. Geez."

"Sorry," Josie said. "I'm still worked up about the lab. I wonder how long it had been since the poor thing had eaten."

"*Beats* me."

Josie glared at me, then frowned and looked down at her lap. She squirmed in her chair.

"That's weird," she said.

"What's the matter?" I said.

"Nothing," she said, standing up to give herself the once over. "I'll be right back."

I watched her head for the ladies room then picked up my wine glass with a big grin on my face.

"Are you going to let me in on what's so funny?" Chief Abrams said.

"Oh, it's just my own version of payback. You heard about the Cessna she chartered for me, right?"

"Of course, I heard about it. It's a small town. You have to admit that it was pretty funny," he said, laughing.

"Yeah, it was a real hoot," I said, making a face at him. "But I've got something even better planned for her. And you can't say a word."

"Hey, I'm a cop. I'm used to keeping secrets."

128

"Okay, then," I said, leaning forward across the table. "I did some searching online for good practical jokes and found an article about some of the jokes George Clooney has played on his friends. And I hit the motherlode with one of them."

"Oh, do tell."

"Josie has been freaking out lately because she believes she's gained a couple of pounds. And since she's always been so proud of the fact that she can eat anything and not gain any weight, Josie's starting to think she might have to cut back, thereby damaging her rather intense love affair with food."

"That's something we all have to deal with as we get older," Chief Abrams said, shrugging.

"Yes, it is. But I'm sort of…accelerating the process."

"How the heck are you doing that?"

"By having her clothes altered."

"What?"

"Yeah, I've started sneaking some of her clothes over to Mrs. Sawyer and having her take in the waistline an eighth of an inch at a time. I'll be doing it a couple times a week. Those are her favorite jeans she's wearing tonight. Judging by her reaction, they're suddenly getting a bit snug around the waist, and it won't be long before she's having trouble with the top button." I sat back in my chair and took a sip of wine. "Pretty clever, huh?"

"I was going to say diabolical."

"Tomato, tomahto."

"She's not gaining weight?"

"Nah, not an ounce. But she doesn't know that. And I can't wait to see the look on her face when she puts her scrubs on tomorrow morning. Okay, here she comes. Not a word."

Josie sat down with a confused look on her face.

"Is everything okay?" I said.

"What? Oh, yeah, I'm fine. Did I miss anything?"

"No, we were just discussing what we were going to have for dessert. If you want the soufflé, you should probably order it now."

"That's okay. I think I might skip dessert tonight."

.

Chapter 18

I was in my office early the next morning with a cup of hot coffee sitting on the desk in front of me and Chloe on my lap trying to make up her mind between two possible resting spots. But if she didn't settle down soon, I was worried that she and the coffee were about to switch places. Eventually, I ran out of patience and gently picked her up and set her down on the floor. She snorted her displeasure then joined Sammy and Jill on the couch. She stretched out between them and gave me the stink eye.

"Did your mama throw you out?" Jill said, stroking Chloe's head.

"She's so spoiled," I said, focusing on the daily schedule in front of me.

"Yeah, like that's her fault," Sammy said. "So, they're coming in to see the Chief this afternoon?"

"Three o'clock," I said, nodding. "It should be interesting. They've already made a mistake."

"Only one?" Sammy said. "I find that hard to believe."

"Well, the day is young, right? They told the Chief they couldn't meet until three because they both worked at night and liked to sleep in."

"And Chief Abrams is going to press them on where they work?" Sammy said.

"You can count on it. And we're going to find out in a hurry how well they think on their feet. It's pretty simple to verify employment."

"I wish I could be there," Sammy said.

"It's better if you aren't," I said, shaking my head. "If we do need your help again, we don't want the Sniffle Twins to have the slightest reason to associate you with the police. Your role is to play the concerned cousin."

"Is this going to get dangerous?" Jill said.

"It could," I said, nodding. "The possibility of being charged with murder and meth distribution could make anybody do something stupid if they got desperate. And for those two, doing something stupid almost seems like a given."

The office door opened, and Josie came in with a confused look on her face. She sat down in a chair on the other side of the desk.

"Sorry I'm late," she said, moving around in the chair trying to get comfortable. "What did I miss?"

"Nothing," I said. "We were just talking about the Sniffle Twins."

"Okay," she said, wiggling in the chair.

"Are you okay, or did you sit on an ant farm?"

"Funny. I'm fine," she said, brushing her hair back from her face. "How does my day look?"

"Not too bad," Jill said, reading from the schedule. "You've got four annual checkups before lunch, and then a spaying this afternoon. That's about it."

"Good. A light Saturday. Works for me," Josie said as she started to drape one leg over the other then changed her mind.

"Okay, if there's nothing else, we'll get going. We've some inventory to count," Sammy said, getting up off the couch.

I gave them a quick wave and watched them head out. Then Josie stretched out on the couch. Chloe draped herself over Josie's stomach and closed her eyes.

"Are you sure you're okay?" I said.

"Yeah, but I do need the number of the company that supplies our uniforms."

"What for?"

"I want to order some new scrubs. These are getting…pretty old."

"They look fine to me," I said, biting my lip to keep from smiling.

"No, they're definitely pretty much finished," Josie said.

"Well, if they aren't *comfortable*, you should definitely get some new ones."

"I didn't say they weren't comfortable. I said they were old. There's a difference."

"Sorry. Geez, somebody's grumpy," I said, getting up and glancing around the office.

"What are you looking for?"

"My CornBelters hat."

I opened the desk drawer where the hat was. I knew this because I'd put it there a half-hour earlier.

"Oh, here it is," I said, putting the hat on. "Right next to the bite-sized Snickers." I held up the bag and shook it. "Fresh bag. You want some?"

"No, thanks. I'll pass."

"You're gonna pass up a full bag of the bite-sized? Are you sick?"

"No. Just a little depressed."

"Well, try not to worry. I'm sure it'll pass," I said, popping one of the bite-sized as I headed for the door. "I'm going to say good morning to the dogs. You want to come along?"

"No. I think I'll just stay here awhile."

I chortled to myself as I headed for the condo area and made a mental note to drop off another bag of clothes with the tailor on my way to Chief Abram's office this afternoon. My first stop was the malnourished lab's condo. The dog was sound asleep as was our summer hire, Jenny. She was in her sleeping bag and had an arm draped over the dog's ribs. The lab's ribcage was still on full display, but it was obvious that the dog was starting to gain some weight. I whistled softly, and both Jenny and the dog opened their eyes. She blinked several times, then sat up.

"Good morning," she said, yawning.

"I brought you some coffee," I said, sliding the condo door open. I handed her the cup then knelt down to pet the lab. "How are you doing, girl?"

"She's doing great," Jenny said, sipping her coffee. "Do you think we can take the IV out today? She's starting to chew on it."

"Let's check with Josie," I said, standing up. "It's her call."

"I'd like to adopt her," Jenny said.

"Josie? Sure, why not? Just remember not to sneak up behind her when she's eating."

Jenny laughed and hugged the dog.

"I think you're perfect for her. What are you going to call her?"

"Sugar. Because she's so sweet."

"I like it," I said, nodding. "Look, I know you've been pulling all-nighters for the past few days, so why don't you take the day off and get some rest?"

"Oh, I'm fine," she said, effortlessly bouncing to her feet.

"It must be nice to be twenty," I said.

"Yeah," she said, grinning. "It is. By the way, I've been wondering something. And I hope you don't mind my asking. How old are you?"

"Slightly north of twenty," I said, heading for the Beezer's condo.

He was sitting on his haunches with his head cocked when I entered the condo. I knelt down, and he greeted me with a lick of my hand, then rested a paw on my knee. I rubbed his head and scratched his ears, then he rolled over and waited for a tummy rub.

"We need to find you a good home, don't we? You must be sick and tired of always being on the move. Maybe a nice big farm so you'll have a lot of room to run. How does that sound?"

Then a light bulb went off. I smiled, filed the idea away, then continued my morning rounds. Two hours later, I'd received way more love and affection than most people probably got in a week, and I headed up to the house to shower and change.

Before I left the house, I removed two pairs of shorts, a pair of slacks, and another pair of jeans from Josie's closet and slipped them into a plastic bag. I made the short drive into town and parked in front of Sawyer's Tailoring & Dry Cleaning. I headed inside, waited for my eyes to adjust to the light, then saw Mrs. Sawyer hunkered down over a sewing machine working on a pair of jeans I recognized immediately. She glanced up and smiled at me, then made her way to the counter.

"Hello, Suzy," she said. "Well, I must say that your plan is working to perfection."

"Those are Josie's jeans, aren't they?"

"Yes, she dropped them off this morning," she said, laughing. "Before she left, she swore me to secrecy."

"She wants you to let them out?" I said, grinning.

"Even better," Mrs. Sawyer said. "She's having me put a piece of elastic in the back."

"I can't believe it. That vain little monster."

"She seemed a bit troubled."

"That's because she's worried she'll have to stop eating half a cow at dinner. Elastic, huh?"

"Yes. It will give her about an extra inch around the waist. And she'll be able to hide it with a belt."

"Perfect. I'll bring them back in a couple of days. Take half of the elastic out."

"I know I shouldn't be enjoying this as much as I am," she said, her eyes sparkling. "But it's so clever. You do know that she is going to pay you back for this."

"Oh, there's no doubt about it," I said, nodding. "Say, Mrs. Sawyer, didn't you say the other day that your grandson was living with you now?"

"Yes, my daughter just went through a very nasty divorce, and they decided to move back to the area."

"How old is your grandson?"

"He's nine."

"How is he handling being out there on your farm?"

"He's doing well, but I do wish he'd start spending a bit more time outside and less in front of his computer playing video games."

"You know what might do the trick?"

"What's that?"

"A dog," I said, smiling at her.

"A dog? Now, that's an interesting idea. We haven't had a dog at the farm since my husband passed. Do you have a specific dog in mind?"

"I do. We found him a few days ago, and he's gorgeous. He's an Ibizan."

"Oh, a Beezer. I'm familiar with them. They love to run and jump around, right?"

"They do. All that acreage you have is just the thing he needs. And the dog will certainly keep your grandson on his toes. And, hopefully, off the computer."

"Does your brain ever stop working?" she said, laughing.

"No, but it definitely has been known to slip a few gears from time to time. What do you say? You're going to love this dog."

"I like it, but I'll need to speak with my daughter and grandson. Can I let you know tomorrow?"

"Of course," I said, handing over the bag of clothes. "Can you have these new alterations done by Monday? I don't want the clothes missing too long from her closet."

"Monday's fine," Mrs. Sawyer said, nodding. "But I do have one question."

"Sure. Go ahead."

"Doesn't Josie have a scale in her bathroom?"

"Yes, she does."

"Then all she needs to do is get on the scale. That would tell her she isn't gaining weight, right?"

"Yes, it would. If she was standing on her own scale."

"I'm afraid you've lost me."

"We bought two identical scales a couple of years ago. Same make and model, but they've never produced the same results. My scale, which is now sitting in Josie's bathroom, has never worked correctly. And it consistently shows a higher number."

"You switched the scales?"

"I did."

"How much heavier does your scale register?"

"Anywhere between four and ten pounds," I said, grinning.

"You are so bad," she said, shaking her head.

"Yeah, I have my moments."

Chapter 19

Chief Abrams roared with laughter, then leaned back in his chair and put his feet up on his desk.

"Elastic, huh?"

"Yeah. I can't wait to see the look on her face when she realizes even that pair of jeans is getting tight," I said.

"She's so gonna make you pay for this one when she finds out. Nice hat, by the way. The Corn*Belters*. The minor leagues always have the best team names."

"They do. Did I mention that Jolene's brother actually plays for them?"

"You did. And you thought you'd wear the hat just to mess with their heads a bit more?"

"Yup."

"Good call. I like it."

"Between the hat and the fact that I'll be sitting here in the police station with you, I imagine they'll have a tough time figuring out what the heck is going on."

"Just don't get too cocky," Chief Abrams said, slipping into the paternal role he occasionally used with me. "Remember what happened to the last person who wore that hat."

We both sat up when he heard the soft knock on the door.

"Come in," Chief Abrams said, getting up out of his chair.

140

Carl and Jolene stepped inside and cautiously looked around. They both flinched when they saw me. Jolene was unable to make eye contact and scratched her arm, the track marks covered by a long-sleeved tee shirt. Carl gave me a menacing glare that left no doubt about what he'd like to do with me but did eventually manage to force a small smile in my direction before focusing on the Chief.

"You must be Carl and Jolene. I'm Chief Abrams. And I believe you've already met, Suzy. Please, have a seat."

"Hi," Jolene said, sitting down on my left.

"How are you holding up?" I said.

"What?"

"Your father?"

"Oh, yeah," she said, shrugging. "You know how it goes. Good days and bad days."

"Of course," I said, nodding sympathetically. "How are you, Carl?"

"Fine."

"She's doing fine," I said, then let my comment hang in the air.

"What?" Carl said, frowning.

"The dog. She's doing fine."

"Oh. Well, that's good, right?"

"Yes, it certainly is."

"That's an interesting hat," Jolene said, scratching the inside of her arm.

"The CornBelters. You gotta love the Cornbelters," I said. "Have you gotten back to Normal to see a game?"

"No," Jolene whispered.

"Well, you should try and make it out there. I'm sure your brother would love to see you."

Jolene flinched, then glanced at Carl who seemed even more perplexed.

"Are you a cop?" he said, looking over at me.

"No, but I'm hoping to play one on TV," I deadpanned.

"Oh. What?"

"Suzy is here because she was the one who discovered the body," Chief Abrams said. "And I thought having a conversation with the three of you might help me put some of the pieces together. You never know when a clue is going to just appear out of thin air. Suzy was just explaining how it was your father's dog that actually found the body."

"Yes, he was," I said, focusing on Jolene. "For whatever reason, whoever killed your dad decided to put his body in a very shallow grave. I guess that made it easier for the dog to find him." I looked over at Carl. "If they had bothered to dig a normal grave, he'd probably still be in the ground."

"Yeah, probably," Jolene said to no one in particular.

"So, I guess we need to thank the dog *and* the killers."

"Thank the killers?" Jolene said, having a lot of trouble processing that idea.

"Yes," I said. "Thank them for either being lazy or incredibly stupid."

"Maybe a bit of both," Chief Abrams said, shrugging.

"Or a whole lot of both," I said, flashing Carl a big grin. "But the dog is the real hero here."

"I hated that dog," Jolene whispered, then her face flushed with embarrassment. "I mean, the dog was crazier than my old man." She coughed and scratched before continuing. "But that's just based on what he told me. Always running around and jumping for no reason. Like the dog wanted to be somewhere else, and that was his way of letting you know. Weird, you know? At least, that's what my father told me."

"I see. And when did he tell you that?" Chief Abrams said, picking up his pen.

"Uh, a long time ago?" Jolene said.

"Okay, got it," Chief Abrams said, scribbling down a note. "A long time ago, question mark."

"Hey, wait a minute," Carl blurted. "Why would talking to us help you figure out who killed Jolene's father? We didn't even know he was around."

"You didn't?" Chief Abrams said, frowning as he flipped back and forth through the pages in his notebook. "Well, how about that? Now, where on earth did I get the idea you did?" He put the notebook down and rubbed his temples. "Maybe my wife is right. Maybe I am getting senile. Well, if you aren't here to talk about the murder, why are you here?"

"The money," Carl said.

"Oh, the money, of course," Chief Abrams said. "The mysterious hundred thousand."

"Do you have it?" Carl said.

"Yeah, I'm sure it's around here somewhere," Chief Abrams said, opening desk drawers one at a time. "Now, where the heck did I put it?"

Jolene's scratching was approaching fever pitch, and I realized that both of them had refrained from getting high before the meeting. But it was getting clearer by the minute that Jolene was starting to regret that decision.

"Are you okay?" I said.

"Yeah, I'm fine," Jolene said. "It's just mosquito bites. Those things love me."

"You must have the good stuff."

"What?"

"Nothing."

"You wouldn't know anybody with the initials TN, would you?" Chief Abrams said.

"No," Carl said. "It doesn't ring a bell. And since nobody knows who this guy is, or I guess it could be a woman, wouldn't the money go to Jolene as the rightful heir?"

"I suppose," Chief Abrams said. "At least it would probably stay in the family. Whatever way Jolene and her brother decide to divide it up would be their call. But I guess that can wait until you actually get your hands on the money, right?"

"Sure, my brother. He can wait." Jolene nodded to herself then focused on Chief Abrams with a confused stare. "So, when can we get the money?"

"Well, you see, that's a bit hard to say at the moment," Chief Abrams said, leaning back in his chair.

"It seems easy enough," Carl said, shrugging. "You hand the envelope over, and we take it."

"Good one," Chief Abrams said, chuckling. "That's funny. No, what I meant to say, Carl, is that, as long as the murder remains an open case, that money is considered evidence. If the case ever goes to trial, the lawyers are gonna need to have it available."

"That's because lawyers are so expensive, right?" Jolene said.

"Well, yes, I'm sure they are, Jolene," Chief Abrams said, turning paternal for a brief moment. "But I was referring to the fact that the money is evidence that would be introduced at the trial."

"Oh, got it," she said with a look on her face that told us she didn't get it at all.

"As such, I'm afraid the money is temporarily on hold. I'm sure you understand."

"So, you're saying we can't get the money today?" Carl said, also beginning to scratch his shirtsleeve.

"Gee, I thought I made my point clear, but maybe not," Chief Abrams said, frowning as he looked over at me. "Wasn't I being clear?"

"No, I got it," I said, nodding. "Loud and clear. An unsolved murder, no money. Solved murder, a hundred grand in the hand."

"Thanks. That's a relief," Chief Abrams said. "If I hadn't been clear, I would have needed to get a checkup just to make sure I wasn't losing it."

"Yeah, nobody wants that to happen," Carl said. "So, you need to find out who killed Jolene's father first?"

"There you go," Chief Abrams said, nodding. "Yeah, it's not my favorite way to spend my time, but crap like that sort of comes with the job. Are you sure you don't have any information that might help me do that?"

Chief Abram's sudden transition, caught Carl off guard and he flinched, then began scratching his arm.

"Do you, Carl?" the Chief said, softly.

"I'm thinking."

While Carl considered his options, I decided to head down a different path.

"How was work last night?" I said to Jolene.

"What?"

"Work. You told Chief Abrams you worked nights."

"I did?"

"No, that was me," Carl said, glancing around with a forced smile. "Yeah, we work nights."

146

"What do you do?" I said, casually.

"Huh?"

"Who do you work for?"

"Uh, what do we do? Who do we work for? Let's see. Oh, we work for...a friend of ours who owns a landscaping business," Carl said.

"You do landscaping?" I said.

"Yes."

"At night?"

I sat back in my chair and snuck a peek at Chief Abrams who was biting down hard on his lip. Jolene and Carl glanced back and forth at each other, then Carl sat up in his chair. Apparently, a neuron had fired.

"We work in the warehouse and help get all the trucks ready for the next day," he said.

Not a bad effort, I decided.

"I see," I said. "So, you don't do any night landscaping?"

"Nah, not in the dark," Carl said.

"But it probably would be a lot cooler at night," Jolene said, scratching hard enough to make Captain and Chloe proud.

"You're probably right, Jolene," I said, momentarily feeling sorry for her. Then I remembered she was a lying junkie who'd almost starved her dog to death and my sympathy evaporated.

"It looks like we're done here, so I guess we should go," Carl said.

"Yes, let's go," Jolene said, almost bolting for the door.

"Thanks for dropping by," Chief Abrams said. "And I wish I had better news for you. But I'll be in touch if anything changes."

"Uh, thanks," Carl said, standing up and giving me one final death stare.

"I'll catch you guys later," I said, giving them a finger wave.

They almost ran to the door and disappeared in a flash.

"What a waste of two lives," Chief Abrams said. "You think they'll get out of the parking lot before they top off the tank?"

"I doubt if they'll make it to the car."

"Landscaping, huh?" he said, laughing.

"Yeah, it looks like he made a good career choice."

"How's that?"

"He seems really good at digging holes for himself," I said.

"Yeah. And I think we're about to find out how bad he is at getting out of them."

Chapter 20

With me behind the wheel, we crossed the Thousand Islands Bridge, chatted briefly with the agent we both knew who was working the line at Canadian Immigration, then headed west on Highway 401. Twenty minutes later, we arrived in Kingston, a city of over 100,000 that had been built at the confluence of Lake Ontario, the Rideau Canal and the St. Lawrence River. My onboard navigation system took us into one of the older sections of the city, and I parked on the street right in front of the address. Chief Abrams glanced at the building to our immediate right and frowned.

"Don't tell me you're hungry already?" he said. "We just ate an hour ago."

"No, that's not it," I said, also frowning. "This is the address I was given."

"Tommy Nostril lives in a diner?"

"There must be a mistake," I said, reaching for my phone. "Hang on." I clicked on the stored number and waited for the call to connect. "Summerman. It's me, Suzy."

"Summerman Lawless?" Chief Abrams said. "Why on earth are you calling him?"

"Long story," I said, then refocused on the call. "Yes, I'm sure you're busy. But I need a quick word with Merlin...Hi, it's me. Suzy Chandler…It's nice to see your mood hasn't improved…Right back at ya." I glanced over at Chief Abrams. "This guy's a real jerk…Nothing. I just said you do really good work. Look, I think you gave me the wrong address. We're sitting in front of a diner…Okay, I'll wait." I glanced over at Chief Abrams. "He said he's checking it again…Yeah, I'm here. You want me to do what?...Okay, I'll get out of the car…Hey, how did you know I was in my car?"

I got out of the car with the phone still pressed against my ear.

"Okay, now what? Take a few steps back? If I do that, I'm liable to get run over by a car…Funny, Merlin." But I took a few steps back into the street, glanced up, and above the awning that extended out from the diner over the sidewalk, I saw the second floor. "Oh, I get it. There's another floor. Probably apartments…Funny. You know, I really don't like you. Yeah, I know, get in line. I'll do that. Thanks."

I put my phone away and gestured for Chief Abrams to join me on the sidewalk.

"There are apartments on the second floor," I said. "What do you think?"

"Well, it is almost lunchtime. And since he lives right upstairs, I imagine the guy eats there from time to time. Maybe we'll get lucky."

"I suppose I could force down a snack," I said, following him into the diner.

It was an old-time diner, and the smell of burgers and onions on the grill was unmistakable. We hung back near the door and glanced around. In a booth near the back of the diner, a solitary man with a nervous twitch was sipping coffee and reading the newspaper. By and large, he was nondescript except for one defining characteristic. He had a huge nose that looked like it had been broken several times, and he kept wiping it with one tissue after another. It appeared he was suffering from a case of terminal post-nasal drip, and I glanced over at Chief Abrams who was already zeroed in on the sniffling man.

"Let's grab that booth in the back," he said, nodding at the one next to the man we both assumed was Tommy Nostril.

I followed him across the diner and slid into the booth. We quickly scanned the menu, and our waitress arrived to take our order. Chief Abrams settled for coffee and a slice of pie. I ordered a cheeseburger and fries. I'd decide later on the pie. He shook his head at me.

"Where do you put it?" he said.

"In my mouth," I said, shrugging. "After that, it usually shows up in all the usual spots. I wish it followed my directions, but it seems to have a mind of its own."

He laughed and put both menus back in the holder sitting next to the condiments. He glanced at me and gestured for me to start.

"Dear," I said, loud enough to be heard in the booth next to us. "Did you happen to see the article in the paper this morning?"

Chief Abrams frowned. I don't think he expected me to open with that question. Or maybe it was the dear that caught him by surprise.

"I don't think so, *dear*. You know I've stopped reading the newspaper. All the news is so depressing. Which article are you talking about?"

"The one about the man they found buried in the woods. In some town called Clay Bay. Do you know where that is?"

We listened closely. I heard the sound of a coffee cup being set down.

"No, I don't. But there must be a lot of small towns around the area," Chief Abrams said. "Which paper did you read it in?"

"I'm not sure," I said. "It might be the local paper here, but I can't remember."

"Well, you only read about a dozen newspapers a day," Chief Abrams said. "It must be hard to keep track of where you've read things."

"I like to stay current, dear."

We fell silent and soon heard the sound of newspaper pages being turned in the adjacent booth. Chief Abrams tucked a finger inside his cheek and tugged it. I nodded; the fish had definitely hit the hook. I made a motion like I was reeling in a fish, and he nodded.

"Anyway," I said. "They found this poor man buried in a shallow grave. Apparently, he died from a massive overdose."

"Tragic. I hate hearing about things like that. That's why I stopped reading the paper."

"Well, maybe you should start again. Anything to get you off your butt and away from that television. I swear you waste more time in front of that thing."

"Hey," Chief Abrams whispered. "Lighten up. You're starting to sound like my wife."

"Good, huh?" I whispered with a grin as I leaned forward. Then I sat back and continued. "But the really interesting thing was the fact that the police found an envelope next to the body that was filled with money."

The sound of pages being turned in the next booth stopped, and I paused for effect.

"That is interesting," Chief Abrams said. "How much money did they find?"

"A hundred thousand dollars."

"Wow. That's a lot of money."

"It certainly is."

"Do the police know who the money belongs to?"

"That's the *really* interesting part. Apparently, the only thing written on the envelope were some initials," I said, my voice rising a notch.

"Initials? Did the article mention what they were?"

"Yes, it did. T. N."

"TN, huh? That's not much to go on," Chief Abrams said.

"Maybe the police are trying to be clever and see if anybody shows up to claim it."

"A hundred thousand in cash? I doubt very much if that money was acquired legally. Who'd be dumb enough to show up at a police station and try to claim it?"

"You're probably right, dear," I said. "But if I were this man, TN, I'd certainly want to know how a hundred thousand of my money ended up next to a dead guy."

"Yes, so would I."

We sat back in the booth as the waitress arrived with our food. She set our plates in front of us and was about to walk away when we heard a voice coming from the booth next to us.

"Check, please."

Chapter 21

At our insistence, Chef Claire had started taking one night off a week, even during the height of the restaurant's busy season. Our nagging had eventually worn her down, and she had agreed that Monday, as the slowest night of the week, was the best option. And that was how Mondays became family dinner night at the house. But Chef Claire was banned from the kitchen the entire evening, leaving the cooking to Josie and me. I was flying solo in the kitchen tonight, and Josie and Chef Claire were in the living room with my mom, a regular on Monday night, and Chief Abrams, whose wife was out of town visiting their grandkids.

I removed the bubbling tray of lasagna from the oven and placed it on the counter to cool, then started working on the vinaigrette for the salad. But it was the smell of freshly baked bread filling the kitchen that put the capstone on dinner hour. I took a sip of wine, grabbed a metal whisk, then paused when I heard the approaching commotion.

"Come on, let's go," Josie said as she opened the kitchen door. "All of you. Outside."

Captain, Chloe, Al and Dente, Bailey, the bloodhound we'd brought back from the Caymans, Winter and Summer, my mom's two mixed basset hounds, and Chief Abrams' basset hound, Wally, padded across the kitchen floor in single file with their heads down. They reluctantly headed outside to the fenced lawn that extended off the back of the house, and Josie closed the door behind them.

"It looked like they were doing a perp walk," I said, laughing.

"For a moment, they forgot who was in charge," she said, shaking her head.

"Well, I guess that's understandable. We are outnumbered," I said, removing two loaves of bread from the oven. "How does that smell?"

"Okay," she said, glancing at the tray of lasagna.

"Just okay? Are you sick?"

"No, I'm fine. I'm just not that hungry tonight," Josie said, checking out the contents of the salad bowl.

"Not hungry? That's lasagna with portabellas and Italian sausage," I said, raising an eyebrow. "Fresh bread and garden salad. No beets."

"Yeah, it sounds good," she said, sighing.

"Your appetite has been off the past several days," I said, feigning great concern. "I'm starting to think we might need to get you to the doctor for a checkup."

"I'm fine."

"If you say so. Hey, are those shorts new?"

"Maybe."

"They look comfy. Elastic waistband and nice and roomy. Good call."

"Yeah, whatever."

She headed back into the living room looking despondent, and I glanced through the window to check on the dogs. All eight were rolling around together on the grass, and I decided that the fresh air would do them good as well as enable us to enjoy our dinner in peace.

Then I caught a glimpse of a section of lawn that was torn up, and a light bulb went off.

I carried everything into the dining room and called everyone to the table. I motioned for Chief Abrams to sit next to me, and I waited for everyone to get settled.

"Remind me to tell you something later," I whispered to Chief Abrams, then addressed the table. "Josie, since the lasagna is right in front of you, why don't you serve yourself, then pass left? I'll follow with the salad," I said, sneaking a peek at Chef Claire who was well aware of what I'd dubbed; *Operation Torment*."

"Fine," Josie said, taking a very small serving of what everyone knew was her favorite lasagna.

She passed the tray to my mother who was staring down at Josie's plate bewildered by what she was seeing. Or rather by what she wasn't seeing; which was a plate overflowing with lasagna. Then Josie put a tiny portion of salad on her plate and waved away the hot bread.

"Are you all right, dear?" my mother said with genuine concern, completely unaware of my diabolical scheme.

"I'm fine. Just not that hungry," she said, casting a loving look at the bread basket.

"Are you sure?" Chef Claire deadpanned. "It looks like something is *weighing heavily* on you."

I glanced down at my plate to hide my grin, then got to work on my salad.

"So, tell us, darling. Where are you and the Chief at with this latest case?"

"Well, we're still testing out some theories," I said, slowly chewing. "Unfortunately, it involves a lot more than just the murder."

"Really?" my mother said, wiping her mouth with her napkin. "This lasagna is magnificent. Well done, Chef Claire."

"Don't thank me," Chef Claire said, nodding at me. "I'm not allowed in the kitchen on Monday nights. This was all Suzy."

"Great job, darling," my mother said. "It's delicious, isn't it, Josie?"

"What's that? Oh, yeah. Delicious," Josie said, toying with her food, then she caught my mother's stare. "What?"

"Who are you? And what have you done with Josie?" my mother said, laughing. Then she looked down the table at me. "Can you tell us what's going on with the case?"

"Geez, I don't know," I said, glancing at Chief Abrams. "Can we?"

"I guess it couldn't hurt," he said, shrugging. "It's not like we have anything concrete at the moment. But let's not get too specific, okay?"

"Got it," I said, already helping myself to a second serving of lasagna that got a soft groan out of Josie. "It appears that the murder is tied in with a crystal meth operation that's working in the area."

"Crystal?" my mother said, scowling. "That stuff is poison."

"Yes, it is," I said. "And we think that Sammy's uncle was somehow involved. We don't have a clue how yet. But we're sure that Sammy's cousin, the dead guy's daughter, and her boyfriend are up to their necks in this thing. They came in for a chat on Saturday, trying to get their hands on a hundred grand that doesn't exist. And yesterday the Chief and I headed over to Kingston to scope out a guy we think is one of the buyers."

"Nice job not getting too specific," Chief Abrams said, shaking his head.

"Yeah, I should probably work on that, huh?" I said, grimacing. "Our best guess at the moment is at least some of the meth is being smuggled into Canada. Probably by boat right out in front of us. And we think the cookers and the buyers are using the woods behind our place as a meeting place."

"What?" my mother said, putting her fork down. "They're using my woods as a place to smuggle crystal meth?"

I stared dumbfounded at my mother.

"Your woods? Are you telling me that you own that property?"

"That's what I'm telling you, darling. I can't believe it."

"Why didn't you ever tell me you owned that land?"

"Darling, if I sat here and told you everything I owned, we'd be here all night."

"When did you buy it?" I said, still stunned by the news.

"It was shortly after you and Josie opened the Inn."

"Why?"

"Because I didn't want anybody building behind your place," she said, gently sliding a forkful of lasagna into her mouth. "And I thought we might want to do something with it in the future."

"Like what?"

"Well, at first, I must admit that I thought it would be a great spot for a golf course," she said, shrugging. "Then I briefly toyed with the idea of turning it into a combination day spa and retreat. You know, a place for people to recharge the batteries. But the numbers didn't work at all. So, I moved to another idea."

"Which is?" I said, raising an eyebrow at her.

"A combination zoo and animal sanctuary," she said, softly.

I let her comment roll around in my head, then grinned.

"You never stop, do you? It wasn't enough to figure out a way to get us to the Caymans in the winter. You're totally committed to making sure I never leave the area, aren't you?"

"Yes, darling, I am. Even after I'm gone, I expect you to be here."

160

I flinched at her reference to mortality but recovered and turned to Chief Abrams. "Remember when you called me diabolical the other day?"

"Sure."

"Well, that's where I get it from," I said, pointing at my mother. "An animal sanctuary? Wow. Now that is a really interesting idea, Mom."

"It certainly is," Josie said.

"Just think about how many visitors a place like that would attract," my mother said. "Not to mention how many year-round jobs it would create."

"It would cost a fortune to build and run a place like that," Chief Abrams said.

"Yes, it will," my mother said. "But we'd set it up as a non-profit, and, if we do have any annual losses, the endowment will cover them. Based on my preliminary numbers, if we're smart, we should be able to at least break even."

"Endowment?" Josie said.

"Yes, dear."

"What endowment?" I said, completely forgetting about eating the rest of my dinner.

"Oh, a little of my money, and some from several friends I've been talking to. But let's not worry about that at the moment. For now, you need to focus on getting rid of the creatures who are selling crystal meth on my property."

161

"Unbelievable," I said, shaking my head in disbelief. "How much land is there?"

"A little over three hundred acres," my mother said. "I can't remember the actual number, but I can check with Rooster if you like."

"Why would you check with Rooster?"

"Because I bought the land from him," my mother said, shrugging. "Actually, he pretty much just gave it away. What's the matter, darling?"

"I was just thinking about money again," I said, spearing a forkful of salad.

"For the hundredth time, it's not money that's the problem. It's what one chooses to do with it."

"And your choice is to build a zoo?"

"Why not?"

I thought about the question, then took another bite of lasagna.

"You know, Mom, at the moment, I can't think of a single reason."

Chapter 22

Despite strong protests from the Chief, I headed out alone the next morning to pay a visit to Larry's Landscaping located a few miles out of town on Route 3. After dinner last night, we'd put our heads together and decided that Carl hadn't come up with the cover story about he and Jolene working at a landscaping company by accident. And after reviewing a list of all the landscaping businesses within a thirty-mile radius, Larry's Landscaping seemed to be the most likely candidate.

First of all, Larry Gentile, the owner, had recently relocated to the area to set up shop. Second, we didn't know anybody who had actually used his services. And in a small town like ours, if people were doing business with Larry's Landscaping, we would have heard about it. Finally, we zeroed in on him because it appeared that Larry did little or no advertising and was apparently relying on word of mouth to generate business. Which led us back to the fact that neither one of us had ever heard anyone talking about the place. We went back to debating Larry's possible motives behind his decision not to advertise, beat that topic to death, then talked some more about the lack of word of mouth.

Then I got a headache and decided to just pay Larry a visit in the morning.

And that was when the Chief started carping about my decision to go alone. When I reminded him about the damage a cop showing up unannounced might do to our investigation, he acquiesced and sent me on my way with a reminder to call him immediately should anything out of the ordinary happen.

I parked between a house and a metal structure that resembled a large garage. But I did see a small sign above the door and knew I was in the right place. I strolled across the dirt parking area and looked around. The house was old, but the structure was definitely new. I walked inside and found the place empty except for bags of fertilizer and mulch and a single truck with the name Larry's Landscaping on the side parked in the back corner. I stood in the center of the room, glanced around, then looked up when I heard a noise coming from the rafters right above where the truck was parked. I listened briefly to what sounded like two men whispering.

"Hello," I called.

"Yeah?" a voice from above said.

"Are you Larry?"

"Who wants to know?" he grumbled.

Nice customer service, I thought. Maybe Larry liked dirt more than people.

"Oh, just a potential customer," I said, deciding to remain pleasant for the moment.

"Hang on," he said, obviously annoyed. "I'll be right down.

I stared up at the rafters, heard some more whispered chatter, then watched him climb down a ladder extending from the back of a platform that sat about twenty feet off the ground. Then I caught a glimpse of somebody ducking behind a stack of white and green plastic bags and shook my head.

"Oh, Carl," I whispered to myself. "What are you doing?"

The grumbling man reached the bottom of the ladder and headed toward me wiping his hands on his pants. When he got close, he extended his hand, and I returned the handshake. He was rail thin and either had a head cold or a head full of something he'd recently inhaled. His fingers were twitching, and the film around his eyes reminded me of a doughnut that had been dipped in glaze.

I had no clue why I was thinking about food at the moment. This guy was a total appetite killer.

"You're Larry?"

"I am. And you are?"

"Looking for someone to do some landscaping at my house," I said, beaming at him. "I'm Suzy."

"Landscaping, huh?" he said, staring at me. "Well, I'll be happy to help, but I'm pretty booked up at the moment."

"That's too bad. How long before you could start work?"

"Gee, I'd have to check my schedule," he said, looking for somewhere to put his hands and ultimately deciding on the back pockets of his jeans. "But it would probably be at least a month. Maybe longer."

"That's a long time to wait," I said, frowning. "Maybe I should look for someone else."

"Well, that's your call," he said, taking a few steps toward the ladder and sneaking a glance up at the rafters. Then he turned around and smiled. "Tell you what, why don't you wait here while I go grab my calendar, and I'll give you an exact start date. That would give you something to work with."

"That would be great," I said, then called out as he started to head for his office. "Oh, and if you could also bring back a few references I could speak to, that would be great."

"References?" he said, stopping and turning around.

"Yeah. Testimonials from a couple of people you've done work for in the past. I always like to check references before I sign any contracts."

"Oh, sure. References," he said, frowning. "Uh, you might have to wait a day or two for those. My computer is on the fritz at the moment."

"Don't you just hate when that happens?"

I watched him head into the office then I heard the unmistakable sound of a cellphone buzzing. I listened to the hushed whispers coming from above, then glanced through the office window and noticed Larry talking to someone on his phone.

"A couple of geniuses at work here," I whispered to myself as I glanced back and forth between the office and the rafters.

The whispers from above stopped, and I snuck a quick glance up at the rafters. One of the bags was being inched partway over the edge of the platform. I recognized the brand since the landscaper who'd done our dog play area had used the same product. It was a fertilizer that came in hundred-pound bags, and I knew that from a height of twenty feet, the impact would probably be enough to kill me if I got hit in the right spot. Like in the head.

Not that I was worried about Carl being able to hit me.

But since it was starting to look like he was definitely going to try, I thought it would be a good idea for me to stay on my toes. Larry came out of the office carrying a large day planner.

"Let's have a look at my schedule," he said. "Say, why don't we do this over at the truck? I think the lighting is better over there."

"Lead the way," I said, following Larry to the back of the truck.

He lowered the tailgate and set the day planner on it. He began flipping through the pages, all of which looked empty.

"No, that week is out," he said, turning the page.

"But there's nothing written on it," I said.

"Yeah, that's because I keep all of it in here," he said, tapping his head.

"Then why do you need a day planner?" I said, casually.

"Uh, for tax purposes?"

"Sure, sure."

Larry kept inching his way to his left, forcing me either to rub up against him or end up positioned right below where the bag of fertilizer was perched above my head. I opted for possible death rather than rubbing shoulders with a twitchy crank head who had a severe case of the sniffles. I took a step to my left. Larry kept flipping through pages and occasionally sneaking a peek over his shoulder up at the rafters. He stopped on another empty page, then tapped it with his finger.

"This is it," Larry said. "The week of the August 15th."

He snuck another glance up at the rafters.

"How does that sound?"

"Geez, the middle of August? That's a long time to wait."

I glanced up, saw a pair of hands reaching for the bag, then shook my head, baffled by the absence of neurons on display.

"I'm really sorry," Larry said, sneaking a final peek up. "It's the best I can do. I really wish…I could…do it now!"

I took a step back underneath the platform and watched as Larry tried to dive for cover under the truck. Unfortunately for Larry, the string of his hooded sweatshirt had somehow gotten wrapped around the tailgate latch, and he struggled to free himself. But a hundred-pound bag of fertilizer, falling from a height of twenty feet, didn't take long to complete its journey. And before I could even try to remember the thirty-two something times something else per second formula used to calculate the speed and force of falling objects, the bag of fertilizer hit Larry on the upper back, drove his chin into the tailgate, then burst open: In the interest of clarity and full disclosure, both his chin and the bag burst. Larry was rendered unconscious on his knees with his chin resting on the edge of the tailgate, bleeding profusely from the mouth, and covered in fertilizer.

"Uh-oh," the voice above me whispered.

"Indeed."

"Man, I'm so sorry, Larry. Larry?"

"Carl?"

"Yeah?"

"I thought you worked nights."

It obviously wasn't what Carl had expected to hear from me, and I waited out a lengthy silence.

"Uh, well, let's see. Larry asked me to come in to help him unload a delivery."

"Of fertilizer?"

"Yeah."

"And you just happened to drop one of the bags?"

"Yeah, that's it. That's what happened. I'm glad you didn't get hurt."

"Me too," I said, stepping out from underneath the platform.

I walked a safe distance away and looked up at Carl who continued to stare down at the unconscious Larry.

"Do you have a phone?" I said.

"What? A phone. Uh, yeah. I think it's around here somewhere. Where the heck did I put my phone? Never mind, I think there's one in the office."

"That's okay. I'll just use mine," I said, reaching into my pocket.

"You calling the cops?"

"The cops? Actually, I thought I'd start with an ambulance."

"Yeah. An ambulance. Good idea," he said, climbing down the ladder.

I made the call, then slid the phone back into my pocket. Carl seemed unsure about his next move, so he settled for a quick scratch as he glanced around the room.

"They said they'll be here in about twenty minutes," I said. "Are you okay?"

"Sure. Why wouldn't I be?" he said with a wide-eyed stare.

"Oh, I don't know. Maybe because you almost killed Larry."

"Accidents happen, right?" he said, apparently testing out the story he was going to try sticking with.

"Yes, they do," I said, glancing around. "Look, I'm late for an appointment. You don't mind waiting for the ambulance by yourself, do you?"

"Oh, no. Not at all. Should I have Larry give you a call?"

"What for?" I said, frowning.

"About the landscaping job. I heard him mention a date around the middle of August."

"I'll let you know," I said, heading for my car. "But I guess we could talk. If he's out of the hospital by then."

Chapter 23

I drove away, made the call, and set my phone in its dashboard holder with it set on speaker.

"Hey," Chief Abrams said. "Have you finished up out there already?"

"Yeah, I wanted to get out of there before the ambulance arrived."

"Ambulance? I'm gonna need a bit more, Suzy."

I told him the story. When I finished, I focused on the road and waited for him to respond. When he didn't, I continued.

"Are you still there, Chief?"

"I'm here. I'm just trying to process what you just told me. He tried to drop a hundred-pound bag of fertilizer on you?"

"Yeah, but he missed and got Larry," I said, slowing down to go past a couple of dogs that were wandering around the edge of the road.

"How bad is the guy hurt?"

"Let's just say that Larry has probably had better days. I'm gonna guess at least a broken jaw and a severe neck injury," I said, accelerating as soon as I could see the dogs in my rear-view mirror. "And a lot of stitches. Oh, and teeth. He's gonna need a whole bunch of new teeth."

"I think I'll wander over there and arrest Carl."

"No, don't do that," I said.

"Why on earth not? He just tried to kill you."

"Yeah, but we'd never be able to prove it. And we want him out walking the streets until this thing plays out, don't we?"

"I guess you're right. But I don't like the idea of somebody thinking they can get away with trying to kill one of my best friends."

"Aren't you sweet," I said as I glanced down at the speedometer and realized I was going eighty. I took my foot off the accelerator and chastised myself.

"What's the matter?" Chief Abrams said, hearing my grumble.

"I think I'm turning into my mother," I said, slowing to sixty.

"You could do a lot worse. You think this guy Larry is handling distribution on our side of the River?" Chief Abrams said.

"Yeah, I do. When you get a chance, see if you can come up with anything about Larry's Landscaping doing work in metropolitan areas."

"Good idea. I'll start with Rochester and Syracuse. If we come up dry with those two, I'll add in Buffalo and Albany."

"My money is on Syracuse," I said. "That's the closest city with a population big enough to support the amount of product they're probably moving. And these guys seem to like doing the least amount of work possible."

"I'll make some calls," Chief Abrams said. "Are you heading home?"

"No, I thought I'd take advantage of Carl being tied up at the moment and pop in on Jolene."

"Interesting. You want some help?"

"Let's keep you out of it for as long as we can," I said. "I thought I'd try *sympathetic confidant*. I can't do that with a cop standing next to me."

"Okay, but call if things get weird."

I laughed into the phone.

"Yeah, let me rephrase that. Call if things get dangerous. We already know it's going to be weird. But who knows, maybe Jolene's dying to chat with somebody other than Carl. She might feel the urge to unburden herself."

"That's what I'm hoping for. She's definitely on the edge, but that could just be all the meth she's doing. But I've been thinking about it, and I don't think she killed her father."

"Maybe not," Chief Abrams said. "But she knows who did. Be careful."

I ended the call and placed another. Josie answered on the second ring.

"Hey," she whispered.

"I'm heading over to see Jolene, so I probably won't be back for another hour or so. How's it going over there?"

"Oh, it's fine."

173

"What's the matter?" I said, grinning. "You sound really down."

"Maybe a little."

"Well, eat something. That'll make you feel better."

"Disagree."

She hung up, and I made a mental note to stop by Mrs. Sawyer's for another round of alterations. I knew I was having way too much fun enjoying Josie's discomfort, but after her stunt with the Cessna, she deserved it. Or at least that's what I told myself with a self-satisfied nod into the rear view mirror.

Then I saw a sign for Defereit and accelerated.

I parked in front of the house and stepped onto the porch. I immediately felt a surge of anger when I saw the spot where the lab had been laying. I knocked on the screen door, and it fell off one of its hinges. I tried putting it back where it belonged, then gave up and knocked on the door behind the screen. The door opened partway, and Jolene frowned and blinked several times when the sunlight hit her eyes. Then she recognized me and opened the door a bit further.

"Suzy, right?"

"Hi, Jolene. How are you doing?"

"Fine. What are you doing here?"

"Oh, I just thought I'd stop by and let you know that Carl might be a little late getting home."

"Good," she said, then caught herself. "I mean, why is that?"

"Larry had a bit of an accident at his place, and Carl is making sure he gets to the hospital."

"What sort of accident?"

"An ill-conceived and poorly executed one."

"What?"

"Nothing. Do you mind if I come in?"

She glanced back over her shoulder, then tried to refocus on me. But she ended up looking past me off into the distance.

"I guess that would be alright. But the place is a bit of a mess," she said, standing aside to let me pass.

"Oh, don't worry about that," I said, stepping inside. "Messy is my middle name."

I stared in disbelief at what can only be described as a Before and After photograph. Before; if taken just prior to the arrival of the demolition crew. After; if shot subsequent to the bomb going off. Then the smell hit me. I glanced around then looked at Jolene who was tossing a variety of items off a chair onto the floor to provide a place for me to sit.

"You guys have a cat?" I said, taking half-breaths.

"No."

"Okay, then," I said, easing myself into the chair.

"You want something to drink?" Jolene said, scratching the inside of her arm. "We got beer and tequila."

"No, I'm good, thanks. I think Larry is going to be okay. Eventually."

"What?" she said, sitting down on an unoccupied corner of a ratty couch. "Oh, Larry, right. What happened to him?"

"I'm sure Carl will tell you all about it."

"I doubt it. He's not much of a talker. Carl's more of a yeller."

"Got it. By the way, where did you two meet?"

"Rehab," she said, scratching her arm harder.

"When was that?"

"When I was in rehab, or when I met Carl?" she said, frowning. Then her face flushed red with embarrassment, and she giggled. "Duh. Same difference, right? It was about two years ago."

"And you moved here right after you met?"

"No, we've bounced around a lot. And I doubt if we're done."

I nodded and glanced around the room, then stared at what looked like dozens of baked beans stuck to one of the walls. It was an interesting pattern, but probably not a decorating choice I would have made.

"Oh, that," Jolene said, following my eyes. "Carl got upset the other night."

"And he threw a pot of baked beans at the wall?"

"Actually, he threw it at me, but he missed," she said, shrugging. "I told him I wasn't going to clean it up."

"Nice to see you sticking to your guns," I said, unable to come up with anything better. "This is really none of my business, but I'm going to ask you anyway. Does Carl hit you, Jolene?"

"Not yet."

"And if he does?"

"He'll be in a world of hurt," she said as a simple statement of fact.

"Maybe it's time you started thinking about doing another stint in rehab," I whispered.

"You sound like my dad," she snapped as her eyes grew wide. She glared at me defiantly. "Are you just offering advice, or are you also going to put on a demonstration?"

"What on earth are you talking about?" I said, bewildered.

Before she could decide how to answer the question, we both heard a car. Jolene got up and started for the door.

"It's probably Carl," she said. "If it is, you should probably get going. He doesn't like you very much."

"Yeah, I kinda figured that out."

I got up and tried to peer through a window. Then I wiped a section of glass with my sleeve and tried again. I noticed the Canadian license plate, then recognized the guy getting out of the car.

"What the heck is he doing here today?" Jolene said, from the doorway before heading outside and closing the door behind her.

I watched her start down the steps and stumble forward. But she caught herself before she fell, and she quickly strode toward the car to meet the man at his car. I pulled my phone out of my pocket and made the call.

"Hey, Chief. It's me."

"Is anything wrong?"

"No, I'm fine. But you'll never guess who just showed up at Jolene's place."

"You're right, I probably wouldn't. Who is it?"

"Tommy Nostril."

"Really? That's interesting. You think he's looking for his hundred grand?"

"That's my first guess," I said, peeking through the window. "They're standing outside by his car."

Jolene was leading an animated discussion, and she pointed at my car, then at the house.

"She just told him that I'm here," I said.

"Are you safe?"

"Yeah, I'm fine."

"Does it look like she's in any danger?"

I continued to watch the scene play out, then made a face when I watched them lock lips for an extended deep kiss. Then Tommy Nostril let his hands roam, and Jolene pressed herself tightly against him.

"Suzy?"

"What?"

"Is Jolene okay?"

"Apart from the risk of catching an infectious disease, I think so."

"What?"

"I'll tell you later. I gotta run."

I slipped my phone back into my pocket and headed for the door, car keys in hand. I bounced down the steps just as they released each other, and both of them studied me closely as I walked toward them.

"I really need to get going," I said, coming to a stop next to Jolene. "Besides, you've got company. Hi, I'm Suzy."

Tommy Nostril returned the handshake and nodded. "How you doin'?"

"I'm good," I said, rocking back and forth on my feet. "If you ever need anything, or want to talk, just give me a call, Jolene."

"What would she need to talk to you about?" Tommy Nostril said.

"Oh, you know, just girl stuff," I said, getting behind the wheel.

I turned the car and slowly headed up the long dirt road. Through the rearview mirror, I saw them heading into the house arm in arm.

"Weird is definitely the word for it," I said to myself when I reached the highway.

I drove slowly and replayed the visit in my head. Her comments about Carl being violent didn't surprise me. And the squalor of the house told me everything I needed to know about her priorities and what little regard she had for her own life. At first, I was taken aback by the fact that she and Tommy Nostril were hooking up, but then remembered they shared a common fondness for crystal. Then I wondered if they might also share a common contempt for all things Carl.

I passed the long stretch of billboard ads for things to see and do in Clay Bay, including one for C's. We still weren't sure if the roadside ad was having any impact on business, but it was something my mother had strongly encouraged us to do. Then I remembered Larry's aversion to advertising and wondered, just for a moment, how he was doing. I returned to my conversation with Jolene and her reaction when I'd gently suggested a return trip to rehab.

Then the neurons in my head exploded. I slowed down and let the idea begin to formulate.

"Put on a demonstration?" I whispered to the windshield.

Chapter 24

Josie stood on the dock, hands on hips, giving me a defiant stare. Captain and Chloe were sitting on the back seat that stretched across the stern, watching her with cocked heads and an expectant look on their face. Captain woofed once at her to hurry up, and Josie glanced down at the Newfie.

"Don't you start," she said, then looked back at me. "I can't believe you agreed to do this without consulting me."

"Relax, it's just dinner. And I'll be there the whole time. Now get in the boat."

"I don't want to go," Josie said, shaking her head like a petulant three-year-old. "Besides, I'm not hungry."

"That's fine. More for me. Now get your butt in the boat."

Josie climbed into the boat, gave both dog's a quick head scratch, then sat down in the seat next to me.

"You look very nice," I said, giving her a small smile. "And you're wearing your favorite jeans."

"Yeah, barely," she whispered.

"What?"

"Nothing."

I hid my grin as I slowly drove the boat to deeper water. I'd picked up the jeans earlier today and put them back in her closet while she was in the shower. As instructed, Mrs. Sawyer had removed half of the elastic she had put in the jeans, and I laughed when I heard Josie grumbling while she was getting dressed.

"Man, is this water level ever going to start going down?" I said. "This is getting ridiculous."

"It certainly is," she said, keeping an eye out for floating objects. "As is the political rhetoric."

"Yeah, the conspiracy theorists are having a field day. They just can't accept the fact that all that rain we've had filled Lake Ontario. And unless I'm missing something, before the water can reach the Atlantic, it has to flow through the St. Lawrence."

"So, it's all Mother Nature's fault?"

"Yes, I'm sure it is," I said, veering around a chunk of wood that was partially submerged. "And for some reason, she's mad at us."

"And you know his how?" Josie said, finally managing a smile.

"Because Mother Nature is just like all the other mothers in the world."

"Is she now?"

"Yes, if you make her really mad, she's liable to do everything she can to make your life miserable."

"Oh, so, you're speaking from experience?" Josie said, laughing.

"Yeah. And I've learned it the hard way."

"I do like her idea of the zoo," Josie said.

"Yeah, me too," I said, nodding. "But let's leave it all to her for now. If she's serious about doing it, she'll just run with the idea. And when she gets laser-focused on something, it's best to stay out of her way. Besides, with our two projects in the Caymans, we've got enough on our plate at the moment."

"Agree," she said, nodding as she stared back out at the water. "I want some penguins."

"Oh, great idea. I love watching those little guys."

"And maybe some stingrays."

"Not a chance," I said, glaring at her.

I pulled into an empty slip in Summerman's boat house, and Josie tied the boat off. Captain and Chloe hopped out of the boat and immediately spotted Murray. They tore down the dock and raced out onto the massive lawn that surrounded the house, a multi-story structure built with stone, wood, and glass. I got out of the boat and waited on the dock for Josie to follow.

"Are you coming?" I said, glancing down at her.

"I'll be up in a minute," she said, tugging at her jeans.

I left the boathouse and followed the path that led up to the house. I stepped onto the wraparound verandah and watched the three dogs roll around on the grass before knocking on the front door. Summerman opened it and beamed at me.

"Hey, I'm glad you made it," he said, glancing around. "Where's Josie?"

"She'll be up in a minute. I think she's making a few last-minute adjustments."

"Okay," Summerman said, confused. "How's she doing?"

"She's really nervous. Please, try to go easy with her."

"Of course. Come on in. Doc and Merlin are in the kitchen. I'm getting dinner ready."

"Merlin, huh?"

"Don't worry, he'll grow on you," he said, laughing.

I followed him down a long hallway and was impressed by the open layout and the high ceilings. A grand piano dominated one of the sitting areas just off the kitchen, and I stepped inside and joined the two men sitting at the granite island. I caught a whiff of something delicious and spotted the vertical rotisserie where a large stack of meat was slowly rotating.

"Suzy," Doc said, pulling the stool next to him out. "It's good to see you."

"Hi, Doc," I said, then glanced to my left. "Hello, Merlin."

"Suzy," Merlin said, cool and distant. "I take it you didn't get run over the other day."

"No thanks to you."

"Did you find who you were looking for?" Merlin said.

"I did."

"You're welcome," Merlin said, taking a sip of what looked like wine then frowning and pushing the glass away. "Geez, this stuff is horrid."

"Yes, it is," Doc said. "They say it's an acquired taste, but I don't think it's gonna happen."

"That sounds like someone I know," I said, glancing at Merlin. "What is it?"

"Retsina," Doc said, also pushing his glass away.

"Yeah, it is pretty bad," Summerman said. "But since we're having Greek food tonight, I thought it was worth a shot."

"It takes like a pine forest smells," Merlin said.

"How about I open a couple bottles of Pinot?" Summerman said.

"Perfect," Doc said.

"I love Greek food," I said, pointing at the rotisserie. "Are we having Gyros?"

"We are," Summerman said, glancing around the counters. "But we have quite a menu. Let's see, what else do we have? For starters, we got Dolmades, Tiropites, Spanakopita, and Tzatziki with fresh Pita. But be careful not to fill up on appetizers."

"Not a chance," I said, casting a loving eye around the assortment.

"The soup course is Avgolemono."

"I'm not familiar with that," I said, frowning.

"It's a chicken soup that finished with an egg-lemon slurry. It's fantastic. And, of course, we have Greek salad. And Moussaka, Pastitsio, and the Gyros for the main meal."

"Don't forget dessert," Doc said, shaking his head at the amount of food in the kitchen.

"Oh, yeah. We have Baklava. And Galaktoboureko. You ever had it?

"No, I haven't," I said, starting to feel very sorry for what I was doing to Josie.

"Well, it's a lot easier to eat than it is to pronounce. It's a Phyllo pie filled with custard and topped with an orange-lemon syrup. It's a total...what's that word you always use?"

"Kneebuckler."

"That's it," Summerman said, pouring wine.

"You must have spent all day in the kitchen," I said, thoroughly impressed.

"Why on earth would I do that?" Summerman said, laughing. "I bought all this."

"Where did you find authentic Greek food?" I said.

"Greece," Summerman said, shrugging.

"Where else do you think we found it?" Merlin said. "Switzerland?"

"I really don't like you," I said, glaring at him.

Merlin shrugged and took a sip of wine.

"I thought you were on the wagon," I said, nodding at his wine glass.

"I am."

"But you're drinking."

"Different wagon," Merlin said.

Doc and Summerman laughed.

"One thing at a time, right, Merlin?" Doc said.

"Exactly."

"When were you in Greece?" I said to Summerman.

"This morning."

Before I could respond, we heard a soft knock on the door.

"Come on in, Josie," Summerman called, heading out of the kitchen.

Moments later, they returned with Summerman staring at her with a concerned expression.

"Is there something wrong with you?" he said, taking a long look at her.

"What are you talking about?"

"Have you been sick?"

"No," Josie said, glancing around at all the food. "Maybe a little depressed."

"Are you sure?" Summerman said with genuine concern.

"Yes, I'm sure," she snapped. "You're kinda freaking me out here, Summerman."

"I'm sorry. It's just that you've lost so much weight."

"Oh, that's really funny. Ha-ha. Good one."

"No, I'm serious. You look like you've lost...I don't know, five, maybe ten pounds."

"I do?" she said, glancing down at herself. "No way."

"C'mon, follow me. I'll prove it to you," he said, leading her down the hallway into one of the bathrooms. "This scale is never wrong."

"Uh-oh," I said after they had left.

"What is it?" Doc said, getting up from the island to grab a tray of Dolmades.

"Well, to put it in terms you'll understand, my cover is about to be blown."

I spent the next few minutes telling them the story. When I finished, I shrugged and grabbed a Dolmades.

"That's brilliant," Doc said, laughing.

"Diabolical," Merlin said, giving me a broad smile. "Maybe there's hope for you yet. You had her clothes altered. I'm gonna steal that one."

"All the credit goes to Mr. Clooney," I said, reaching for another of the stuffed grape leaves.

Josie came out of the bathroom with an odd mixture of delight and anger plastered on her face.

"You're behind this, aren't you?" she said.

"Behind what?" I said, coyly, then couldn't hold back my laughter. "Yeah. As payback for the Cessna." I beamed at her. "You have to admit that it was pretty clever."

"I'll admit to nothing. You've been messing with my clothes, haven't you?"

"Yup. And I also switched scales with you at the house."

"I knew my face was getting thinner, but I chalked it up to depression."

"Are you mad?" I said, grinning at her.

"Oh, yeah. Of course, I'm mad. But I'm sure I'll get over it," she said, then paused for effect. "Just as soon as I get even."

"Okay, thanks for the warning," I said, taking a sip of wine. "For now, how about we just enjoy our dinner? Take a look at this delicious feast. You must be starving."

"I could eat."

Chapter 25

Josie was sitting on the couch in my office with her feet up on the coffee table, Captain's head in her lap, and a rapidly disappearing bag of bite-sized Snickers in her right hand. She was using the other hand and her teeth to open each one and toss them into her mouth like she was eating popcorn. The impressive and highly efficient display she was putting on was like watching an artist at work. Like Picasso. Or maybe, judging by the collection of wrappers strewn all over the floor, Jackson Pollock.

"Nice to see that you've fully recovered from your recent eating disorder," I deadpanned.

"Shut it."

My phone rang, and I checked the number, then answered and set the phone down on my desk.

"Hi, Tony. Thanks for calling me back."

"No problem, Suzy. How are you doing?"

"I'm good. Everything's good. And Sammy says hi. How are you hitting these days?"

"Not bad," Tony said through the phone. "Still having a bit of trouble laying off low and away, but definitely a lot better. What's up?"

"Hang on a sec," I said, glancing up when I heard the soft knock.

The office door opened, and Chief Abrams entered. We gave me a quick wave, then sat down on the couch next to Josie. He frowned at the wrappers spread all over the floor.

"Welcome back," he said, chuckling.

"Don't start," Josie said, tossing what was left of the bag of bite sized into a drawer.

"You have to admit it was a stroke of genius," he said, gesturing for me to continue with my call.

"I'll admit to nothing."

"Okay, I'm back, Tony. I won't keep you. I just have a couple of questions about your dad and sister," I said into the phone.

"I'm happy to talk about my father. But I really don't have much to say about Jolene."

"Sure, I get that," I said. "Okay, this is going to sound really invasive, but was your dad a heavy drug user?"

"No, I seriously doubt it…apart from the anti-psychotic stuff his doctors had him on. If he didn't stay on them, he sort of…left the planet. But when it came to street drugs, he was adamant about us staying away from them. That's where most of the problems he had with Jolene came from. Did you manage to track her down yet?"

"Yes, we have," I said, softly.

"Is she still using?"

"Oh, yeah. And in very high doses. I'm sorry."

"Meth?"

"At a minimum."

191

"Meth was always her favorite. How bad off is she?"

I couldn't help but pick up on the tone of his voice. Instead of coming across as worried, he sounded more like he was on a fact-finding mission: Interested, but definitely not overly concerned.

"She seems to be going downhill and picking up speed. No pun intended," I said. "And her boyfriend is a cooker."

"Then it looks like she hit a home run with him," he said, casually. "An endless supply, huh?"

"Yes, for now anyway. Do you know her boyfriend? He's kinda tall, really skinny, probably around thirty years old. His name is Carl."

"No, I stopped trying to keep track of the men coming and going through her life years ago. That was a full-time job all by itself. But like I told you when you were out here, Jolene and I haven't spoken in a long time. Have you or the police figured out who killed my father?"

"Not yet, but I think we might be getting close," I said.

"Was Jolene somehow involved?"

"I'm not sure," I said. "But I think the operative word here is *somehow*. I'm afraid that it's a definite possibility."

Tony fell silent, and I waited it out. Eventually, I continued.

"Are you okay, Tony?"

"I don't really have much choice, do I? Oh, by the way, thanks for sending my dad's ashes. They arrived the other day."

It was my turn for silence. *You're welcome* just didn't seem to cut it. I decided to cycle back.

"Did your sister ever mention a guy by the name of Larry Gentile? He's a landscaper, or at least he plays one in real life."

"That's funny," Tony said, laughing. "Plays one in real life. I need to remember that one. Larry Gentile? No, I got nothing. About the only guy I do remember was her steady boyfriend back in high school."

"Okay, thanks," I said, about to end the call.

"What a piece of work he was. Jolene was a freshman, and this guy was older, a dropout I think. He was the one who got her started using in the first place. Boy, did my dad hate him."

"I'm sure your dad hated most of the guys she hung out with," I said, checking my watch.

"Yeah, he did. But my dad saved most of his hatred for this guy," Tony said, with a soft chuckle. "Man, Tommy Hoover. I haven't thought about that guy in years."

"Excuse me? What did you say his name was?"

"Tommy Hoover, like the vacuum cleaner. In fact, that was his nickname. The Vacuum."

"The Vacuum?" I said, light bulbs popping all over the place. "Was the nickname a reference to all the drugs he did?"

"As a matter of fact, it was," Tony said. "He was well-known for his ability to inhale rather large quantities of powdery substances."

193

"Because of the size of his nose, right?" I said, staring at Chief Abrams.

"How the heck did you know that?"

"Lucky guess," I said, leaning back in my chair. "Do you know what happened to the guy?"

"I have no idea," Tony said. "I always figured he ended up like most of Jolene's other friends. Either dead or in jail. Hey, I need to get going. We've got an afternoon game, and I'm late for batting practice. Let me know if you find out anything more, okay?"

"Will do," I said. "Thanks, Tony."

I ended the call and frowned as I glanced over at Chief Abrams.

"Coincidence?" he said, raising an eyebrow at me.

"What? Jolene just happens to end up in the same location with a guy who fits the description of her old boyfriend? Based on what I saw going on between them this afternoon, I'd put the probability of it being a coincidence somewhere around zero."

"My sentiments exactly," Chief Abrams said. "Jolene and Tommy Nostril might be the masterminds behind all of this? That's a scary thought."

"Her brain is obviously fried," I said. "But that wasn't always the case. Tony mentioned how much potential she had when she was younger. And then she just wasted it. Can you check to see what sort of criminal record Tommy Hoover has?"

"I already sent a text," Chief Abrams said. "It shouldn't take long to get it."

"It must be coming up on ten years they've been together, right?" I said.

"That sounds about right," he said, checking his phone. "Nothing yet."

"Jolene said that she's been with Carl a couple of years. That must mean they like to keep swapping out cookers. You know, not sticking with the same one for too long."

"Or finding a new one after the previous one gets caught," Chief Abrams said.

"Now, there's a thought," I said, nodding. "Jolene said she met Carl in rehab."

"What better place to find someone who cooks meth?" Chief Abrams said.

"You're saying she checks herself in and out of rehab whenever they need to find a new cooker?" Josie said, gently tapping Captain's head who was snoring loudly. "Hey, we're trying to talk here." Captain opened one eye, snorted, then fell back asleep.

"I don't know if that's what I'm talking about or not," Chief Abrams said. "It does sound strange when you say it like that."

"Yes, it does," Josie said. "Plus, you're forgetting one important question. If all the previous cookers she's been with have been caught, why the heck isn't Jolene spending the next several years wearing an orange jumpsuit?"

"I have no idea," Chief Abrams said. "She certainly isn't someone who covers her tracks very well."

"Pun intended?" Josie said with a grin.

Chief Abrams chuckled and looked over at me.

"What do you think, Snoopmeister? Why isn't Jolene behind bars?"

It didn't happen that often, but, occasionally, my subconscious took control of my mouth.

"Because she's being protected," I blurted, then frowned at my outburst.

"Jolene? An informant?" Chief Abrams said. "Man, if that's the case, the Feds must be desperate."

"Both of them are snitches," I said. "Her and Tommy Nostril. That has to be it."

"How on earth could you possibly know that?" he said.

I looked at Chief Abrams as I flashed back to Summerman's admonition about keeping my mouth shut. When I had agreed to do that, I thought that keeping his secret would be simple. Now that I was seeing how various situations were playing out, as well as the preponderance of potential problems woven into it, I was beginning to have my doubts. I broke eye contact and shrugged.

"Lucky guess?"

"Nice try," he said, maintaining his intense stare.

I was rescued when his phone buzzed. He glanced down at it, then began scrolling through the message. Several moments later, he looked up and gave me another odd stare.

196

"Tommy Hoover has a long list of priors," he said, glancing back down at the message. "Several for possession, plus the usual suspects...several B&Es, he stole half a dozen cars, knocked over some gas stations and liquor stores. All before the age of twenty-three."

"And since then?" I said.

"Nothing. Not a thing since 2006."

"Sounds like something you'd expect to see on an informant's file," I said.

"Yes, it does," Chief Abrams said. "You got something you want to tell me, Suzy?"

"No, I don't think so," I said, glancing out the window. "Could you check Jolene's record?"

"Way ahead of you. I pulled it the other day. Two charges of possession. The first time she got off with a warning. She got probation for the second. Six months. And there was another charge for solicitation. She paid a fine and was released. There's been nothing since then. Take a guess what year it was the last time she got arrested."

"I'm going to go with 2006 for a thousand, Alex," I said.

"Nothing gets past you," he said, laughing.

"How could they be informants?" Josie said. "From what you've told me about them, it sounds like they're lucky if they're able to find their shoes in the morning."

"I'm gonna go out on a limb and guess that you've never spent much time around informants," the Chief said. "Not a lot of Harvard grads living in that swamp."

"If they've been informants for ten years, they might have convinced themselves they're untouchable," I said.

"That would be my guess. At some point, they probably got cocky and decided to bend the rules and branch out a little," Chief Abrams said. "And they got away with it and just kept going."

"And the Feds just let them cook and smuggle crystal meth?" Josie said.

"It would probably depend on what they're working on," Chief Abrams said. "If it's a big enough case, the Feds might look the other way."

"Or maybe the Feds have forgotten about them and don't have a clue what they're up to," I said.

"It's possible, but I have my doubts," Chief Abrams said. "The Feds are a lot of things, but forgetful isn't one of them."

"They could be getting paid for snitching on other druggies?" Josie said.

"Sure," the Chief said, shrugging. "If they're heavily involved, they could even be on a retainer."

"Our tax dollars at work," Josie said, shaking her head. "The government spends our money protecting people like that?"

"Try not to think about it," I said.

"Why not?"

"Because it'll just give you a headache."

Chapter 26

That afternoon was another reminder why Josie and I do what we do. Any day when we are able to witness one of our dogs being adopted into a loving family is enough to put a lump in our throats, watching two on the same day always got us reaching for a box of tissues. The first adoption dealt with the lab we'd found starving to death on Jolene and Carl's front porch. Jenny, one of our summer hires, had continued to bond with the dog, and the two of them had become inseparable during the dog's recovery period. She was sitting on the floor of the dog's condo next to Josie who was doing one final check of the Lab's vital signs. Josie listened to the dog's breathing through a stethoscope, then lovingly stroked the dog's head, and stood up.

"I now pronounce you woman and best friend," she said, removing the stethoscope from her ears. "She needs to put a few more pounds on, but she's perfect. Make sure she gets her daily exercise, but don't overdo it the first week."

"Thanks, Josie. You too, Suzy," Jenny said, hugging the dog.

"You did most of the work," Josie said. "Now, why don't you take the rest of the day off and get her settled into her new home?"

"Are you sure?"

"Go," I said, laughing. "And feel free to bring her with you when you come to work."

"Really?"

"Yeah, in case you haven't noticed," Josie said. "We have a pretty loose policy when it comes to dogs in the office."

"Thanks so much. You guys are the best," Jenny said. "You ready to go home, Sugar?"

"Love the name," Josie said, nodding.

We watched her head out the back door using a leash the dog didn't need and waved as she drove off. We headed into reception and found Mrs. Sawyer sitting with her daughter and grandson. She smiled at me but gave Josie a cautious look, unsure of the reception she was going to receive from her.

"Hi, Mrs. Sawyer," I said, then glanced at her grandson. "You must be Billy."

"That's me," he said, bouncing excitedly on his chair.

"We have someone very special for you," I said.

"I can't wait," the boy said, literally starting to bounce off his chair.

I was glad to see how much energy the boy had. He was going to need every bit of it to keep up with the Beezer.

"Hello, Josie," Mrs. Sawyer said.

"Hi, Mrs. Sawyer," Josie said, giving nothing away. "It's nice to see that you could get away for a while."

"What's that, dear? Oh, yes. I wouldn't have missed this."

"Of course," Josie said, giving her a small smile. "And I'm sure your fingers could use the rest."

"I'm sorry, Josie," she said, managing a nervous chuckle. "But it was so clever, I couldn't resist. You have to admit that it was one of the funniest practical jokes you've ever seen."

"I'll admit to nothing," Josie said, then cracked a genuine smile. "Don't worry, Mrs. Sawyer. Any and all retribution will be directed at the evil woman standing next to me."

"Now I'm evil?"

"On a good day," she said, then turned to the boy. "Why don't you and your mom come with me? There's somebody who's dying to meet you."

I watched them head toward the condos then sat down next to Mrs. Sawyer.

"She's still mad, isn't she?"

"A little," I said. "But it pales in comparison to how happy she is to be eating again."

"What do you think she's going to do?"

"I have no idea," I said, laughing. "I imagine she'll take her time, and just when I think she's forgotten all about it, she'll strike. Like a cobra."

"I swear, you two," she said, shaking her head. "Do you have any special instructions about the dog?"

"Josie is covering all that with them right now," I said. "But just make sure that your grandson and the dog spend as much time together as possible the first several days. The dog's been through a lot and is going to be disoriented until he gets used to being around the farm. But as soon as he bonds with your grandson, he won't want to leave his side. Remember though, the breed loves to run and can really jump. With the size of your farm, I doubt very much if he's going to take off and get lost. As long as your grandson makes that bond happen. Don't feel bad about reminding him about that for as long as you need to."

"I'll do that," Mrs. Sawyer said.

Soon, the grandson came through the door holding the end of a leash. The Beezer was excited and definitely ready to get outside. Josie gave the boy's mother a few final instructions, then we waved goodbye. Josie gave Mrs. Sawyer a hug on her way out and whispered something in her ear.

"What did you say to her?" I said after they had left.

"None of your business."

"Don't you dare do anything to her."

"Relax," Josie said, gently punching me on the arm. "I would never to do anything to that sweet woman."

"Good. I wouldn't want her to be a victim of whatever you decide to do."

"Victim? Never. Try to think of her as more of an *accomplice*."

She headed to her next appointment with a big grin on her face that made me nervous. Then I shrugged.

"It was still worth it."

Chapter 27

It was late, at least two-thirty in the morning, and was I sitting in the lounge at C's chatting with Doc and listening to Summerman work his way through an intricate piece of music I couldn't have mastered if I had eight hands and a lifetime to practice.

"How does he do that?" I said to Doc.

"I have no idea. It's a world I'm not familiar with."

Doc felt my stare and glanced over at me.

"I'm talking about the music world. Not the other thing."

"Got it," I said, nodding. "Thanks for agreeing to talk to Tommy Nostril today."

"No problem. The Nostril and I go way back."

"How does he seem now compared with the way you remember him from the old days?"

"Old, and in the way," Doc said, shrugging.

"Funny," I said, glancing over at him. "That's a little harsh, wouldn't you say?"

"No."

"Was he surprised to see you?"

"Oh, yeah," Doc said, grinning. "He certainly was. And I've always made him nervous."

"Do you enjoy making people nervous?"

203

"Only people like the Nostril."

"Did he ask why you just happened to show up unannounced?"

"No, over the years he's learned not to ask me that question."

"Because he's afraid of what you might do to him, right?"

"Do you show up with a list of prepared questions, or do they just come to you?" he said, shaking his head.

"What do you think?" I deadpanned. That got a small grin out of him. "Did he buy your story?"

"Of course, he bought it," Doc said, frowning at me. "I do this stuff for a living, and I'm very good at it."

"There's no need to get snarky. I was just asking," I said, focusing on the music. Then I couldn't help myself. "So, I was right about the Feds pretty much forgetting about Carl and Jolene?"

"Yes, it looks like you were," Doc said. "It happens from time to time. One of his handlers retired. Then the DEA made some changes to the way they were structured and what various sections were responsible for. Another agency he was snitching for had him flagged in their database as dead. Over time, everybody just sort of forgot about the Nostril. And when they did, it appears that Tommy decided to *seize the day* and start moving a lot of product," Doc chuckled. "And like most informants, Tommy never felt the need to reach out to them to update them on his whereabouts."

"Sounds pretty incompetent," I said, yawning as I sat back in my seat.

"Not necessarily," Doc said. "The bureaucracy is huge and often impossible to navigate. And they're trying to keep track of millions of people. That creates a lot of opportunities."

"I'm not following you."

"If the government didn't have some things they couldn't do themselves, people like me would be out of work."

"What exactly do you do for the government, Doc?" I said, raising an eyebrow at him.

"I just told you. Pretty much anything they can't do by themselves without a lot of people asking questions they don't want to answer."

"Gee, thanks, Doc. That narrows it down. Plausible deniability, right?"

"Yeah, that's the term they like to use," Doc said, shrugging. "I don't know why. Nobody ever believes them when they do."

I laughed and sipped my Limoncello then tucked my legs under me. I pushed my hair back from my face, then caught him staring at me. My face flushed red, and I blamed the two glasses of wine I'd had with dinner. I continued to watch his stare out of the corner of my eye, then turned to him.

"What?"

"I was just sitting here thinking about what a great addition you'd be to our little team," Doc said.

"That's all you were thinking?"

"That's all I'm going to admit to for the moment."

I turned an even deeper shade of red and set my Limoncello down on the table in front of me.

"Your idea of reaching out to the Nostril was brilliant," Doc said, raising his glass in salute.

"Thanks," I said, focusing on my breathing. "So, he was surprised to see you?"

"You're starting to repeat yourself. Yeah, he was surprised at first. But I have a tendency to pop in on people when they least expect it, so he got over it in a hurry."

"Were you able to work what we talked about into your conversation?" I said.

"You mean the part about how the local cops were starting to zero in on him?"

"Yeah."

"I did mention it in passing," Doc said, grinning. "Then I gently suggested that he might want to find a new place to set up shop after his next shipment arrives."

"He didn't happen to mention when that was scheduled for, did he?"

"No, he didn't. But I suppose I could help you find out."

"No, you've done a lot to help, but you need to back out. You can't be around when this goes down."

"When it *goes down*?" he said, frowning.

"Yeah, I watch a ton of cop shows," I said, shrugging. "If you were around, Chief Abrams would start asking a lot of questions

206

that could lead back to Summerman's situation. And I gave him my word."

"Okay, I get that. But you need to be careful. The Nostril might be a total crank head, but he's still dangerous."

"Sure, sure. How did the Nostril react when you told him that the police had turned over the hundred grand to Carl?"

"Not well," Doc said, enjoying the memory. "He grabbed his fork so hard it bent in half, then his eyes started rolling around in his head. I imagine he'll be reaching out to Carl soon to schedule a meeting."

"I'm sure he won't have any problem getting Carl to agree," I said, giving him a coy smile.

"What did you do, Suzy?"

"I asked Chief Abrams to call Carl today and tell him that he was able to track down the guy whose initials were on the envelope. Carl did everything he could to get Chief to divulge the name, but he wouldn't do it. But Chief sprinkled a ton of hints about who it was that will be easier to follow than a trail of breadcrumbs."

"And you think that Carl is worried the police are going to give the money to the mysterious TN?"

"Yes, I do. I imagine it's very much on his mind these days."

"I'm impressed," Doc said. "What about Jolene?"

"What about her?" I said.

"Aren't you going to concoct a story to get her attention?"

"No, I don't think we need to do that. I'm afraid she's on her last legs, and she's so incoherent at the moment, I don't want to confuse her any more than she already is. The way I see it, Tommy is going to reach out to her and tell her that Carl has the hundred grand. Then when she confronts Carl about it, thinking he's cutting her out of the deal, Carl is going to deny it and tell her that the cops told him that Tommy is about to get his hands on the money. Either way, Jolene's going to be convinced that one of them is lying to her."

"But both of them will be telling her the truth, at least what they think is the truth."

"Yeah, that's one of my favorite parts," I said, allowing myself another sip of Limoncello.

"And if you can get the three of them together talking about it, all you need is some witnesses, preferably the law enforcement kind, to overhear it."

"Yeah, that's pretty much it," I said, nodding. "What do you think?"

"Well, I probably wouldn't go to all that trouble. I'd just shoot them," he said, shrugging. "But that's just me. And you think that's the way you're going to figure out who killed Jolene's father?"

"Oh, I've already figured out how he died," I said. "My biggest concern is putting a stop to them running drugs through those woods. If I don't, my mother is gonna kill me."

"Your mother?"

"Yeah. And we need to get them out of there so we can start working on the zoo," I said, flashing him a quick smile.

"Zoo," Doc said, flatly. "You know, Suzy, every time I start thinking I'd like to ask you out, you…"

"Say something weird?"

"Weird might be a bit harsh, but, yeah."

"I should probably start working on that," I said, nervously crunching on an ice cube. "You really want to ask me out?"

"I said I was starting to think about it," Doc said. "But I'm worried about being too old for you."

"In case you're wondering, I'm somewhere north of twenty," I said, glancing over at him.

"How about that? Me too."

"Just like the Arctic Circle is somewhere north of the equator?" I deadpanned.

"Funny."

Chapter 28

I parked near the edge of the woods about a quarter-mile downwind from Jolene and Carl's place and opened the driver side window and the sunroof. I took a deep breath, only got a heavy dose of pine, then relaxed into my seat. After three nights of what Josie and Chef Claire were calling *utter nonsense*, I had to admit that I was beginning to wonder if they might be right.

But, to me, my logic remained unassailable. Working backward from the problem, I had ended up parked amid the pines, defending myself against hordes of mosquitos and the occasional curious skunk, sniffing the air for telltale signs of meth being cooked. The way I saw it, the final confrontation in the woods would have to happen soon. Based on everything Doc had told me, the Nostril wouldn't leave the area until he got his hands on the final shipment. And he couldn't do that until Carl did some serious cooking. As soon as the meth was cooked, Tommy and Carl, who were both dying to get their hands on the hundred grand, would want to do the exchange as soon as possible. And Jolene, desperate to find out which one of the two men in her life was trying to screw her on the deal, would definitely be coming along for the ride. Convinced that we'd planted more than enough seeds to sow some serious contempt among the three of them, all we needed to do was figure out when the cash for crystal deal was going to happen. But because the number of mosquitos in the woods behind the Inn outnumbered the ones I was currently dealing with by at least ten to one, Chief Abrams and I weren't about to begin our stakeout until we were sure the new shipment had been cooked.

Chief Abrams and I were convinced that, as long as we were careful, we'd be able to handle the three crank heads. We weren't concerned about the possibility of Larry the Landscaper showing up. He was still in the hospital wearing a horse collar around his neck and drinking his meals through a straw.

I stuck my head out the window and took another deep breath. All I got was another heavy hit of pine.

And a hint of chicken.

I'd been expecting Josie to wait awhile before she sought revenge, but I'd misread her. Knowing of my fondness for taking really hot showers, Josie had somehow managed to stuff several bouillon cubes inside my shower head. And when I got in the shower earlier today, I soon found myself soaping up amid a steamy chicken broth that, while easy to wash off my body, had proved impossible to get out of my hair. I'd eventually managed to share a fake laugh with her about it, then I immediately headed to the kitchen to bake a batch of chocolate cupcakes stuffed with a delightful beet-yogurt filling I invented on the spot. I'd left the cupcakes in her office and headed out before she found them.

I congratulated myself for being incredibly clever and decided to celebrate with a snack while I waited for the smell of cat urine to start wafting in through the open sunroof. I rummaged through my backpack for the bag of Double Stuffed Oreos that was still half full. I took a sip of water then popped one of the Oreos into my mouth. I chewed hard, got a heavy dose of a familiar but unpleasant flavor, then spit all over my steering wheel. I climbed out of the car and spent the next few minutes taking sips of water and spitting on the ground until the taste of toothpaste subsided. Knowing when I was in over my head, I decided calling a truce with Josie would be the first item on our agenda at tomorrow morning's staff meeting.

My phone buzzed, and I climbed back in the car, set the phone in its dashboard holder, and started wiping down my steering wheel.

"Hey, Chief."

"What are you doing?"

"Apparently discovering new ways to brush my teeth."

"What?"

"Nothing. What's up?"

"Just checking in. Any signs of them cooking yet?"

"No, but it's still early," I said. "As soon as I do, I'll give you a call."

"Great. If it's not too late by then, I'll give Jolene a call and ask her to stop my office in the morning. I'd like you to be there. How does your day look?"

"I've got a meeting with one of our sales reps at nine, but I should be able to slip out after that."

"You sure this is the way you want to go?" he said. "We could just go ahead and arrest her on the spot."

"We've waited this long, so let's see if we can wrap the whole thing up in one shot."

"I guess."

"You sound troubled, Chief."

"I'm just not used to holding off on making arrests this long. It makes me nervous."

"You just don't want to sit in the woods all night and get eaten alive," I said, laughing, then cocked my head. "Hang on a sec." I took a deep breath and caught a heavy whiff of something that smelled like a dozen cats had been trapped inside a confined space for several days. "Bingo."

"You smell something?"

"I do. I'm getting a heavy dose of cat pee…and a touch of chicken and Colgate."

"What?"

"Long story," I said, closing the sunroof and the window. "Okay, they're definitely cooking. Go ahead and give Jolene a call. Have her come in around ten. I should be able to get there by then."

"Okay, will do. Now, why don't you head home and get some sleep?" Then he laughed into the phone. "Maybe take a nice long hot shower."

"She told you?"

"She did. With great delight."

213

"That shrew."

"You might want to let it go. You're pretty relentless when you put your mind to it, but she's tenacious," he said, still laughing. "But now that I think about it, perhaps you should share the experience with others. Who knows, maybe you'll get a Chicken Soup for the Soul book deal out of it."

"You're pretty funny for a cop."

"Agree."

Chapter 29

The next morning Josie and I bantered back and forth during our morning meeting, congratulated ourselves on our ability to be diabolically clever when necessary, then sealed our new truce with a pinky swear. Then I argued with a sales rep about the price he was trying to charge us for dog shampoo and other supplies, wore him down to a nub, then headed for the Chief's office.

Jolene was already sitting across from him sipping a cup of coffee. I said hello to the Chief, glanced around to confirm she'd come alone, then sat down next to her.

"How you doing, Jolene?" I said.

"I'm okay," she managed with great effort.

I couldn't believe how much worse she looked than the last time I'd seen her a few days ago. She seemed worn out, both inside and out, wasted away past the point of no return. Her face was shrunken, and the skin was beginning to sag on her arms. Her eyes were red, she seemed to be having trouble catching her breath, and she had a vacant stare that, despite her many despicable life choices, made me feel sorry for her. I felt even worse knowing what we were about to do to her.

"Okay," Chief Abrams said. "Let's get started. Thanks again for coming in, Jolene."

"Yeah, no problem," she said, scratching her arms harder than Chloe did when she was on the hunt for a flea. "You said you had some information about my father?"

"Yes, I believe we do," the Chief said. "And just so you know, I have no intention of arresting you this morning."

A neuron fired somewhere in her head, and her eyes came into focus.

"Arrest me? Why would you do that?"

"I'm not," he said, shrugging. "I just wanted to let you know that in case you were worried."

"Well, I wasn't," she said, staring across the desk. "Until you mentioned it."

"Forget I said anything," he said, sitting back and relaxing.

"Easy for you to say," she said, sniffling then wiping her nose with a quick swipe of her sleeve. "So, what do you have to tell me?"

"Before I get to that," the Chief said. "I'd like to clear up a few things if that's okay with you."

She shrugged and let her eyes drift. Chief Abrams nodded at me.

"Jolene," I said, softly, then waited for her to focus on me. "Tell me a bit about your father."

"What do you want to know?"

"Your brother mentioned that your dad had some serious mental problems he was dealing with," I said, turning toward her.

"Yeah, what about them?"

216

"Tony said that he could function unless he went off his medication."

"Medications. Plural. He was on more drugs than I...ever imagined possible."

"Got it," I said, glancing at the Chief.

"Tony also said that he lost touch with your father after your mom died. He said your dad started moving around a lot but never let him know where he was or where he was going next."

"That's because Tony was always the chosen one." Jolene shrugged, then adopted a mocking tone. "Did you hear about Tony? Tony made all-conference. Tony got straight A's. Tony this, Tony that." She paused to catch her breath. "No, he never worried about Tony."

"Because he thought Tony didn't need his help?" I said, choosing my words very carefully.

"Probably."

"But he was worried about you, wasn't he?"

Jolene stared at me, and tears started rolling down her cheeks. Chief Abrams handed her a box of tissues, and she brushed at her eyes with a handful. Then she wiped and blew her nose. The Chief slid the trash basket closer to her then sat back in his chair.

"Yeah," she eventually whispered.

"Your dad was following you and Carl around the country, wasn't he?" I said.

"How did you know that?" she said, wide-eyed.

217

"In all honesty, it's the only logical explanation I could come up with. I mean, for a reason why he would have been hanging around here."

"He wouldn't leave us alone," she whispered. "No matter how hard I tried to get him to go away."

"Your dad kept showing up trying to convince you to…." I didn't want to let her know we knew about her and Tommy's relationship. "To get away from Carl. And the drugs."

"Yes."

"And your father being around here was just one more time he happened to show up unannounced, wasn't it?"

"Yeah. But it had to stop. It had been going on for a long time. No matter how many times I moved, he'd always find a way to track me down. I don't know how he did it, especially with the shape he was in."

"And he felt the same way as you, right?"

"About what?" she said, confused.

"That it needed to stop," I whispered.

She nodded, deep in thought.

"And he finally got tired of trying to talk you out of quitting, didn't he?"

She nodded again, and I noticed tears beginning to collect in a small pool in front of her chair.

"So, he decided to *put on a demonstration*."

"How did you know that?"

"You mentioned it to me the other day when I stopped by your house?"

"I did?" she said, frowning.

"At the time, you were mad at me and asked if I was going to put on a demonstration. It didn't make any sense to me at first, then it came to me."

"I didn't kill my father," she said as the sobs started and her chest began to heave. "Not directly."

"I know you didn't, Jolene. The night you and Carl were in the woods, he showed up, didn't he?"

"Yes, he did."

"You and Carl were probably out there having a little fun, maybe doing the romance thing," I said, feeling small for having to lie to her. "And when your father saw what sort of shape you were in, he decided to *demonstrate* what he thought you looked like when you were high on meth. He wanted you to see it for yourself, right?"

"As if I don't know what I look like. It's pretty hard to miss. He *poured* half a bag of crystal into his mouth," she said, cringing at the memory. "I couldn't believe he did that."

"Then what happened?" I said, fighting back my own tears as I tried to get to the end of the conversation as quickly as possible.

"He swallowed hard to get it all down, then he started ranting and raving like he always did, then he stood real still for a long time then just collapsed on the ground. I kept waiting for him to

219

get up," she said, staring off into the distance, replaying the scene in her head I imagined, then she exhaled loudly. "But he never did."

I glanced at the Chief, completely spent. I shook my head and did some staring off into the distance of my own.

"Jolene," the Chief said softly. He waited until she focused on him then continued. "Whose idea was it to bury your father in the woods?"

"Does it really matter?"

"Yes, I'm afraid it does," Chief Abrams said, sitting forward and putting his elbows on the desk.

She nodded and remained silent a very long time. I wondered if she was trying to decide which of the two men in her life was lying to her about the imaginary hundred grand. Then I wondered if she had finally decided to just come clean and tell the truth. And it was right around the time when I started thinking that she might not even remember whose idea it had been that my headache started. I did my best to shut my neurons down and let things play themselves out. Eventually, she looked at Chief, started to lean forward to speak, then changed her mind and closed her mouth tight. Then she finally continued.

"It was…*Carl's* idea."

"I see," Chief Abrams said, sitting back in his chair.

"Are you going to arrest him?"

"No, not at the moment," he said, glancing at me.

"Well, if you plan to, you better hurry. We're leaving town tomorrow," she said, suddenly focused and apparently intent on throwing Carl under the bus.

"Where are you going?" I said.

"Probably back to rehab," she said.

"That sounds like a good idea," I said.

"It's what I always do when I…get this bad," she said, shrugging. Then her neurons coalesced on a single thought, and her eyes briefly came alive. "What about the money?"

Every ounce of sympathy I'd been able to summon for her disappeared in a flash.

"The money? Didn't Carl tell you about it?" the Chief said.

"He told me some story about how you had tracked down the guy with the initials TN and planned on giving it to him," she said, staring hard at the Chief. "But I don't think I believe him."

"I see. Well, I think that's a conversation for you and Carl to have," the Chief said, glancing at his watch. "Suzy, we're running late."

"Oh, that's right," I said, playing along and getting to my feet. "We better get going."

"I'm sorry, Jolene," the Chief said. "But I really need to run. Why don't you chat with Carl, and then if you still have questions, stop by in the morning before you leave town?"

"But I need to know if I can believe Carl," she said, grudgingly getting up from her chair and following us to the door.

"I'm sure you'll figure it out," the Chief said, stepping outside into bright sunlight.

Jolene squinted and shielded her eyes with her hands as if the sun was attacking her. We walked to my car and left her by herself on the sidewalk.

"But what about the money?" she called out. "Hello? What about my money?"

We climbed in the car, and I backed out of the parking spot and drove away with no specific destination in mind. I turned Miles Davis on low and let soft trumpet wash over me. Apart from ratcheting up my melancholy mood, it didn't help.

"That was pretty despicable on our part, wasn't it?"

"Not one of our finer moments," he said, staring out through the windshield.

"It was kinda like kicking a puppy."

"Yeah. Not a part of the job I enjoy very much."

"She almost had me. Right up to the point when she started worrying about the money."

"Yeah, I know, but I'm trying to cut her some slack. She's a very sick woman," he said, turning up the music.

"She's way past sick," I said, turning left for no particular reason. "She's dying."

Chapter 30

It was Josie's turn to make Monday dinner that evening. But, rest assured, before I began working my way through the Shepherd's Pie, I carefully examined what was on my plate and waited until she had taken a few bites. Then, and only then, did I start eating. We might have called a truce, but I'd been burned before.

"Are you sure you don't mind keeping an eye out for the Nostril's boat?" I said.

"No, we got it covered," Josie said.

"We're going to do it in half-hour shifts," Chef Claire said. "From the living room using binoculars."

"You sure you don't want to watch from outside?" I said. "Maybe down by the dock?"

"No, as much as we hate disappointing all the mosquitos, the living room will work just fine," Josie said.

"Okay. Thanks for doing that. Text me as soon as you see anything."

"You're sure it's going to happen tonight?" Josie said.

"Yes, we are," Chief Abrams said as he helped himself to another serving. "This is fantastic, Josie."

"Thanks," she said, then turned serious. "Please don't do anything stupid tonight. Like getting shot."

"Don't worry," the Chief said. "We're going to hang back in the woods while it plays out. The state police will be covering the shoreline as well as the dirt road where Jolene and Carl parked the last time. Nobody will even know we're there."

"Except the mosquitos," Chef Claire said. "You better slather up before you head out."

The Chief and I both held up the containers of bug repellent we were carrying then slid them back into our pocket. Josie and Chef Claire waved off our offer to help wash up, and we headed outside.

We walked down to the Inn, across the dog's play area, then out through the gate on the far side. As we approached the woods, Chief turned on his flashlight and shined it down at the ground as we carefully made our way to the spot where Jolene's father had been buried. We came to a stop near the gravesite, and I followed the beam of the Chief's flashlight as we decided where to hide. We needed a place where we could hear the conversation, but not be seen. I pointed to a familiar spot behind a large rock about thirty feet away from where we were standing.

"Right over there," I said. "It's perfect."

"How on earth would you know that?" the Chief said, shining the light in my eyes.

"Don't do that," I said, waving the beam away. "I'm not one of your perps."

"Sorry, force of habit, I guess," he said, laughing.

"And to answer your question, I know it's a good spot because I've used it before."

"Really? Oh, please, do tell."

"I was in high school. And a lot of kids used these woods."

"I see. A little late-night romp in the woods under a full moon?"

"It sounds a lot more romantic than it is," I said. "Trust me, the only thing bare skin does out here is serve as an invitation to them to move in."

"Them?" the Chief said, laughing as his voice rose a notch. "You been holding out on me, Suzy?"

"No, you idiot. I was referring to the mosquitos."

"Oh, the mosquitos. I see. So, you weren't talking about your former boyfriends."

"No, I most certainly wasn't," I snapped.

"Because they'd already been invited, right?"

"Shut it."

He followed me to a soft grassy spot behind the rock laughing the entire way. I ignored him and spread a blanket out on the grass and sat down to check the sight lines. Chief Abrams sat down next to me, set the flashlight on the blanket, and left it on as he checked his phone.

"The state police are in place in both spots," he said, slapping his arm. "Here they come. I hate these things."

"Put some more repellent on."

"Good idea," he said, rubbing both arms with the lotion. "Oh, you'll be pleased to know that we tracked down a bunch of information about Larry the Landscaper."

"Did you get enough to put him away?"

"Oh, yeah. Not only has he been a major distributor in Syracuse, but it also looks like all the cooking supplies that Carl has been using were purchased through Larry's company. He's toast."

"Good. Did you ever find anybody he did landscaping for?" I said, also applying another round of repellent.

"Not a single person," the Chief said, shaking his head.

"Have the state police got a confession out of him?" I said, reaching for the bag of bite-sized I'd brought along.

"No, thanks. I'm good for now," he said, waving away the bag. "They did. Apparently, when Larry came out of his morphine haze, he took one look at the charges he was facing and tried to make a deal. He gave up Carl without breaking a sweat."

"What about Jolene?" I said as my phone buzzed.

"No, he didn't mention her. Or Tommy Nostril," the Chief said. "The cops think he and Jolene might have had a little thing going on. And they're pretty sure Larry doesn't know the Nostril."

"Okay, Chef Claire just texted me," I said, glancing up from my phone. "The Nostril's boat just went past our place."

"We better get settled in then," he said, turning off the flashlight.

In the darkness, the only sound we could hear was the rustling of pine boughs in the breeze that was beginning to stiffen. And the mouse-like crinkle of the bite-sized wrappers.

"You might want to put the bag away," Chief Abrams whispered.

"This is my last one," I said, through a mouthful of chocolate. "You sure you don't want one?"

"Maybe later."

We stretched out on our stomachs next to each other peering around opposite sides of the rock in front of us. Moments later, we saw the beam of a flashlight sweeping back and forth across the path we'd just traveled. Then we heard the sound of a car off in the distance to our left, followed by the sound of two doors closing. I held my binoculars up to my eyes and was able to identify the Nostril. He was dressed in black from head to toe, and a small backpack was draped over one shoulder. He had the flashlight pointed down at the ground and was waving his free hand around to keep the mosquitos at bay. Then he gave up and put a hand in his pocket then pulled it out holding a gun. Without removing the binoculars from my eyes, I punched Chief Abrams in the shoulder.

"Ow. Knock it off," he whispered. "I see it."

"I doubt if he plans on shooting mosquitos."

"Shhhh. Here come the Sniffle Twins."

I focused the binoculars on Carl and Jolene who were approaching from the other direction. Carl was also carrying a backpack, and he seemed angry. Jolene stumbled her way along the path looking even worse than she had this morning. Carl came to a stop about fifteen feet away from Tommy Nostril, and they glared at each other. Carl must have noticed the gun in the Nostril's hand because he reached into his coat to retrieve one of his own. Both men continued to glare each other with their guns pointed down at the ground. Carl handed Jolene the backpack he was carrying, and she staggered briefly under the weight when she grabbed it. Uncertain where to stand, she eventually settled for standing halfway between the two men. She was facing us, and even in the dim light, I could tell she was having a hard time remaining upright.

"Okay," Carl said to the Nostril. "I need to count the money. Toss it over."

"Let me see the product first," the Nostril said, shining his flashlight on Jolene.

She squinted, then set the backpack on the ground and removed two large bundles wrapped in clear plastic. She held them up for the Nostril to see and waited for further instructions.

"Ten kilos," Carl said. "Just like we agreed. Okay, throw me the money."

The Nostril tossed his backpack on the ground directly in front of Carl. He knelt, quickly counted the bundles of cash, then stood and glared at Tommy.

"Where's the other hundred grand?" Carl said.

"You mean the hundred grand the cops gave you the other day?" the Nostril said. "Nice try."

"What are you talking about?"

"I heard all about it. I know you have it. And since that envelope had my initials on it, I'd like it back," the Nostril said.

As they argued back and forth, I focused on Jolene who listened to the two men, then sat down on the ground.

"Did either one of you stop to wonder how my father got his hands on a hundred thousand dollars?" Jolene said to no one in particular.

"Good question," I whispered to Chief Abrams.

"Yeah, it's a little late to be asking it though."

"Stay out of this, Jolene," Carl snapped.

"Don't talk to her like that," the Nostril said. "Apologize."

"What?" Carl said, frowning at the Nostril.

"I said apologize."

"For what?"

"Geez, when it comes to you, where would I start?" the Nostril said, laughing. "Don't worry about him, Jolene. Consider the source."

"I don't worry about anything," Jolene said, then she started laughing. "Never have, never will."

"Shut up, Jolene," Carl said. "You're starting to be a real a pain to have around."

The Nostril slowly raised his gun and pointed it at Carl's head.

229

"Okay. Now I'm going to have to insist on that apology," the Nostril said. "Why don't you get up off the ground and come over here, Jolene?"

"Are we done playing *who's got the hundred grand?*" she said, reaching for one of the meth bundles.

"Come on over here, baby," the Nostril said.

"Why would she do that?" Carl said, glancing back and forth at them with a confused look on his face. "And don't call her baby."

"You're such an idiot," the Nostril said. "Come on, Jolene. Right over here."

"She's not going anywhere," Carl said, raising his pistol at the Nostril. "Especially with you."

"Don't point that thing at me unless you plan on using it," the Nostril said.

"Oh, don't worry, I'm gonna use it."

Then two shots fired at close range rang out and echoed through the woods. Carl and the Nostril stared at each other, then dropped their guns and fell to their knees. They remained in that position looking at each other, stunned. Then they both fell forward face down on the ground.

"That's gonna make my job a whole lot easier," the Chief said, glancing over at me.

I started to get up, but Chief Abrams pulled me back.

"Just wait a sec," he whispered.

I focused on Jolene through the binoculars, and she seemed dazed, even oblivious to what had just happened. Then she noticed the Nostril's flashlight on the ground and picked it up. She stood, pointed the light at the two bodies on the ground then cocked her head.

"Carl? Tommy?"

"She's completely out of it," the Chief whispered.

It was the biggest understatement I'd ever heard in my life.

She stumbled forward toward the bodies staring down at them. Jolene whimpered like an injured puppy and wandered around in a small circle. Then she did something that would haunt me for months to come. She searched the burlap bag she was using as a purse and removed a small pocketknife. She struggled to open it, then picked up one of the meth bundles and sliced it down the middle. I watched her stumble back to the bodies and empty the contents of the bag all over both men. When they were covered with the white powder, she tossed the plastic on the ground and giggled hysterically.

"Good batch, huh?" she said, glancing around before spotting the second bundle. "Okay, let's finish this once and for all."

"What's she talking about?" I whispered.

"I have no idea."

Jolene dropped the flashlight on the ground, and she stood framed in the light as she picked up the second bundle and sliced it down the middle with the knife. But instead of spreading it over the two bodies on the ground, she held it up over her head and poured it into her mouth. As soon as I realized what she was doing, I burst out from behind the rock and raced toward her. By the time I got to her, she was on the ground choking and gagging. A white foam streamed out of her mouth, and her eyes were blinking rapidly.

"Jolene," I said as I slid underneath her on the ground and held her in my arms, shocked by how little she weighed. "Jolene." I slapped her face, and her eyelids fluttered before she managed to focus on me.

"Suzy?"

"Yes, it's me."

"What are you doing here?" she whispered, then swallowed hard. "Wow. What a rush."

"C'mon, Jolene," I said, shaking her shoulders. "Hang on. We're going to get you some help."

"No, I'm fine," she whispered as she closed her eyes. "This is…the way it had to go."

"Jolene," I said as I continued to vigorously shake her. "Come on. Hang in there."

"Shhh."

The sound she produced reminded me of air being let out of a tire. I felt her body start to relax, then she came to and opened her eyes.

"I got a question."

"Sure. Go ahead," I said, glancing up at Chief Abrams who was standing next to me.

232

"There never was a hundred grand, was there?"

"No, Jolene," I whispered. "There wasn't."

"I knew it," she whispered, managing a small grin. "Well played."

My stomach sunk, and my eyes filled with tears as I again felt her begin to drift away.

And then she was gone.

Epilogue

Well played. I spent the next three days in bed tormented by Jolene's final words. I replayed those final moments dozens of times with the curtains closed, soft jazz playing, and Chloe by my side. The only useful thing I did was have an extended phone call with Tony. We talked at length about his sister's life, her poor choices, and her death. He'd been surprised to hear that Tommy Hoover had still been in the picture, and was baffled by the possibility that his sister might have been a government informant at one point in her life. He asked me to make arrangements, like I'd done with his father, to have her ashes shipped to him. I agreed and was relieved when he stopped short of asking me to explain Jolene's motivations or lack thereof: I had nothing to offer. We ended the call with a mutual promise to stay in touch. I gave the probability of that happening no better than a 50-50 shot.

It wasn't because I didn't like Tony, it was quite the opposite in fact, but I knew that every time I saw him, or even spoke on the phone, his sister's death, and the role I'd played in it, would come rushing back to haunt me. Everyone, especially Chief Abrams, scoffed whenever I mentioned that I was at least partially responsible for Jolene's death. I eventually agreed they had a point, and my obsession with the idea faded into my subconscious.

But it continued to surface and nag at me from time to time like a wound that would not heal.

Over time, I got back into the swing of things and rededicated myself to our work at the Inn. We expanded our rescue program, Josie and I finally finished the presentation we were scheduled to present at an upcoming conference, and my mother and her architect completed an initial set of plans for the zoo and animal sanctuary. All of us had written off her idea as just of those late-at-night wine conversations people tend to have. But when she showed us the plans and mentioned she was already in discussions with a zoo in China about taking a few Yak off their hands, we started to believe her.

I should have known better. Doubting my mother's resolve to get something done only made her more determined to prove all the skeptics wrong. Not to mention it really ticked her off.

We even managed to find some time to enjoy the River. The water level had peaked and had begun to recede in early July, but it remained high throughout the summer. I decided that Mother Nature, while still angry with us, was starting to cool off. But the high water didn't stop us from doing a little fishing and taking all five house-dogs out for frequent swims in the Lake of the Isles.

Josie and Summerman were still at an impasse, but they'd at least figured out a way to be in the same room together without her bursting into tears. Merlin continued to be a thorn in my side, and Doc and I continued to flirt whenever we saw each other. But before we could discover if it was ever going to go anywhere, he, along with Summerman and Merlin, headed off to an undisclosed location and were gone for most of July and all of August. When Summerman did arrive back in the islands, he came alone. And as the official last day of summer approached, I, once again, started making plans for being there when Summerman crossed back over.

I guess some things in life need to be seen more than once before you believe they're possible.

On the day before he crossed over, I headed into reception just as Jenny was arriving for work. Sugar, the starving lab we'd rescued, bounced through the front door and headed straight for me. I knelt down and rubbed the dog's head, then patted her stomach and glanced up at Jenny.

"She's turning into a little chubster," I said, shaking my head. "Aren't you, Sugar?"

The dog rolled over onto her back and kicked her legs in the air.

"You're kinda proving my point," I said, laughing as I rubbed the dog's belly.

"Is she getting too heavy?" Jenny said, frowning.

"No, she's good, but keep an eye on her weight," I said, standing up.

"I have a hard time saying no to her," Jenny said.

"Occupational hazard," I said, glancing over at Sammy who was standing behind the counter studying the computer. "Sammy, I need to run out for a while."

"No problem," he said, glancing up. "Hey, I talked with Tony this morning. He said to say hi."

I flinched, then forced a smile and grabbed my car keys from my pocket.

"How's he doing?" I said, pausing at the front door.

"He's okay, but he said this is his last year of playing ball."

"Really?" I said, walking over to the counter. "Why is he quitting?"

"He said the dream is over. But he's okay with it. He said something about outer space I didn't get, and then he said something even weirder."

"What was that?"

"He said you would understand better than anybody else why he was walking away."

I frowned as I thought about it, then I smiled.

"Shoot for the stars. You might only end up on the moon, but you'll still be in a place only a handful of people have ever seen."

"Yeah, that was it," Sammy said. "You really said that to him?"

"I did."

"That's pretty good advice."

"Yeah, I have my moments."

I thought about Jolene and her complete lack of dreams about what might be possible for her to achieve in life and my stomach dropped. I flashed back to that night in the woods, and could almost feel her birdlike body in my arms. *Well played.* Sammy caught the look on my face.

"Are you all right? All of a sudden you seem really sad."

"I'll be okay."

Then I whistled softly, and Chloe came tearing into reception wagging her tail furiously and staring up at me.

"See? Problem solved," I said to Sammy as I rubbed her head. "You want to go for a ride?"

Chloe raised up on her back legs and tapped the car keys with one of her front paws.

"I think she likes the idea."

We went for a long drive through the back roads with no particular destination in mind. We had the windows and sunroof open, and Chloe seemed to sigh contentedly whenever the cool breeze hit her face. After putting a hundred miles of destination-free mileage on the car, we slowly made our way home for a night in front of the TV with Josie. All five house-dogs slept soundly in front of the fireplace while we sipped wine, sort of watched a bad rom-com, and, in general, just caught up. I slept soundly with Chloe stretched out next to me, and I woke fully prepared for the last day of summer.

I spent most of the day thinking up ways to stay busy, and around six PM I hopped in the boat by myself and made my way to Summerman's island. The wind was down and the early evening air was warm, and I lovingly glanced around at the fall foliage.

As expected, I heard piano music coming from the library, and I was greeted by Murray as soon as I stepped out of the boathouse. The dog had an extra bounce in his step, and he led the way as I strolled toward the screen door. Murray tapped it with his paw, caught the partially open door with his head, then waited for me. I pulled it open, and the dog dashed inside and draped himself across Summerman's feet underneath the piano.

"Hello, Suzy," he said, continuing to play. "Why am I not surprised to see you here?"

"I guess I'm a slow learner," I said, sitting down on the couch.

"Not exactly how I'd describe you, but whatever floats your boat, right?"

"I have a few more questions."

"I'm shocked," he said with a grin as he attempted what looked like the piano version of a triple somersault. "Dang it. I almost had it. What's your question?"

"You mentioned that on the day of your accident, that it was Paco, your grandmother's partner, who managed to bring you back to life."

"You're slipping, Suzy," he said, trying the complicated run up the keyboard again. "That's not a question."

"Funny. I was wondering what ever happened to him and your grandmother."

He attempted the run a third time, executed it to perfection, then grinned down at the keyboard. "Finally. It took me all afternoon to get that right." Then he closed the lid and glanced over. "Okay, I'm all yours. What was your question?"

"What happened to your grandmother and Paco?"

"Would you like the truth, or do you want the easy answer?" he said, staring at me.

"The truth, of course."

"Okay, but you should be careful what you wish for," he said, getting up from the piano and sitting down next to me on the couch. "A few years ago, they...transitioned."

"Transitioned?" I said, frowning. "What the heck does that mean?"

"I have no idea," he said, shaking his head. "I still can't believe it myself. But Murray and I watched it with our eyes right on the verandah up at the house. Didn't we, Murray?"

The dog woofed once and trotted over and stretched out across Summerman's feet.

"You mean, they crossed over, right? Like you do?"

"No, this was different," he whispered. "And transitioned is the best word I've come up with to describe it."

"Transitioned into what?"

"Two of the most beautiful bald eagles you've ever seen," he whispered.

"C'mon, Summerman. If you don't want to tell me, just say so," I said with a grin.

"No, I'm not joking. Paco was Native American and very famous in his tribe for being what you and I might call a shaman."

"Okay, yeah, I get it," I said, laughing and wiggling my fingers at him. "Booga-Booga. He was able to turn himself into an eagle. And take your grandmother with him."

"There are a lot of things going on around us we don't understand. I thought that someone who asks as many questions as you do would get that. And Doc is convinced that you're someone who's definitely on the path to enlightenment."

"Doc said that?"

"Doc's a Buddhist," Summerman said with a shrug.

"He is?"

"Yeah, but he's not sure he's a very good one. I guess we were both wrong. Maybe you aren't an inquisitive seeker of knowledge. Maybe you're just nosy."

"Geez, Summerman," I said, scowling. "You might want to cut me some slack. I just started to get my head around your situation, and now you're telling me about some sweet old couple who turned themselves into bald eagles."

"If you watch the sky closely, you'll probably see them later while Murray and I are crossing over."

"No, it's not possible," I said, shaking my head vigorously. "I don't believe it."

"You aren't going to throw up, are you?"

"No, I don't think so."

"Well, if you do, either try to make it to the bathroom or go outside before you do," he said, laughing. "Cleaning that up is not how I want to spend my last few minutes on this side."

241

"I'll do my best. Bald eagles? There must be some mistake."

"Mistake. Miracle. Mystery. Take your pick. They all work," he said, getting up off the couch. "Okay, Murray. Are you ready?"

The dog bounced to his feet and began rapidly pacing back and forth.

"I think he likes the idea," Summerman said, laughing.

"Yeah, I recognize the look."

"Suzy, I have to say that it's been a pleasure seeing you this summer. And I'm sure we will be seeing lots more of each other when I get back next year. Be sure to say hi to Josie for me. We didn't quite get as far as I hoped we would, but I think we might be on the right track."

I stood, and he gave me a long hug.

"Try to stay out of trouble," he said.

"Yeah, you too," I said, shrugging.

"I never have to worry about that over there," he said, starting to disrobe. "You're welcome to stay, but if you watch me get naked, I just might be forced to hover in on you while you're showering."

"Don't you dare," I said, flushing red with embarrassment. "I'll see myself out. Take care of yourself. And this big guy as well."

I gave Murray one final head scratch then waved goodbye to Summerman and headed for my boat just as the sun was slowly beginning to sink below the horizon. I backed out of the boathouse and headed about five hundred yards upriver Then I turned the boat off and drifted just as Summerman and Murray began their swim toward the main channel. I watched them through the binoculars and saw the smile on his face and the dog's tongue lolling around his mouth. When Summerman reached his departure point, he started to backstroke and waved to me. I lowered the binoculars, waved back, then waited until they submerged and didn't return to the surface.

I shook my head, again amazed by what I'd just seen, then remembered. I glanced up at the sky and saw two magnificent eagles soaring about a hundred feet above the water. They swooped down close to the surface, seemed to tip their wings in salute, then flew right over my boat as if checking out the uninvited stranger. They soared until they became a speck in the early evening sky and disappeared.

Dazed, I leaned over the side of the boat and threw up. I wiped my mouth, took a sip of water, and waited until my stomach settled. Then I sat down behind the wheel and started the boat to head for home. I eased the throttle forward, alternating glances out at the main channel and up at the sky. Seconds later I came to an abrupt stop when I hit the shoal that extended off the island near the library. My boat bounced along the top of the shoal and then came to a sudden stop when I heard the unmistakable sound of my lower unit being sheared off. I turned the engine off and glanced over the side to find myself, for the second time this summer, drydocked in the middle of the River.

"Unfrigginbelievable," I said, shaking my head as I checked for damage.

Satisfied that the boat wasn't leaking, I reached for my phone, took one final look up at evening sky, and placed the call.

While I waited for it to connect, I took a moment to reflect on the wonder of life.

About all the choices, both good and bad, we make during our brief time on this side.

And the opportunities we miss simply by not paying close enough attention when they present themselves.

Not to mention the problems you can run into when you take your eye off the ball.

Like the big chunk of submerged rock my boat was perched on at the moment.

Well played, indeed.

My call was finally answered on the fifth ring.

"Hey, Rooster. You're never gonna guess what just happened."

www.ingramcontent.com/pod-product-compliance
Lightning Source LLC
Chambersburg PA
CBHW070743180626
46818CB00007B/2971